FOREVER HER VISCOUNT

DUKES MOST WANTED
BOOK FIVE

❧

SCARLETT SCOTT

HEA
Happily Ever After Books

Forever Her Viscount

Dukes Most Wanted Book Five

For Christi - thank you for uplifting me, inspiring me, supporting me, writing with me, laughing with me when I need it most, and serving as a daily reminder of what a real friendship is and always should be.

I'm so thankful to know you and call you friend.

CHAPTER 1

*N*eville Astley, fifteenth Viscount Wilton, hated most people.

While he abhorred social gatherings of every sort, no abomination was quite as hideously wretched to endure as the country house party. To him, country house parties were the equivalent of walking barefoot through the wilds of Scotland in the coldest depths of winter. He'd rather subject himself to any other form of torture. But for his elder brother's only daughter, he would do anything, even if it meant playing life-sized lawn chess in Yorkshire or being chased by an irate swan. Even if it meant listening to dreadful singing and playing companion to a potted palm during a ball.

Even if it meant inadvertently catching Lady Charity Manners swimming in nothing but her chemise during his customary early-morning walk.

He hadn't intended to linger when he first heard the rhythmic sound of water splashing. Nor when he'd discovered the tidy heap of feminine garments that suggested whoever was swimming was not just a lady, but also one who was wearing shockingly little.

She wasn't completely naked as she emerged from the sparkling Sherborne Manor lake just now, the chemise plastered lovingly over the contours of her well-curved form. But she may as well have been. Before him stood the most compelling evidence that the rumor about the scandalous nude Venus painting was true. Because she looked every bit as glorious and beautiful as the picture he'd seen on display at the Grosvenor Gallery.

She had posed for it.

He was certain.

The knowledge was astonishing. He couldn't fathom the daring she must possess. Not just to sit naked for the painting's lurid depiction of the goddess, but to swim at a house party wearing a garment that was essentially transparent.

Neville was horrified. He was also—and quite against his better judgment—moved. Every part of her was perfectly formed, a temptation he couldn't seem to stop devouring with his gaze, even though the gentleman in him knew he ought to look away.

"Lord Wilton," she said brightly, as if they had met under ordinary circumstances and he couldn't see her nipples through that wet scrap of linen. "You're taking your morning walk early today."

He was, by half an hour.

How the devil did she know? More importantly, why was she not making any move to cover herself?

"You ought to dress, Lady Charity," he said stiffly. "For the sake of your modesty."

Where was her chaperone? She had come to the house party with her aunt, Lady Louise Manners. The woman clearly had no notion what manner of mischief her charge was making. Either way, Lady Charity was fortunate that it was Neville who had happened upon her and not one of the other guests.

She shrugged carelessly as she wrung water from her hair. "Haven't you heard? I don't have any modesty."

Of course he had heard. Everyone in England had heard. But he'd never bothered to mire himself in speculation and gossip. Nor had he given much thought to a woman he'd supposed he would never meet.

"Perhaps you should have some," he countered in the same stern voice he used for his beloved niece whenever she was rebellious.

Which, unfortunately for Neville, was frequently.

In the wake of his elder brother's and sister-in-law's deaths over a year ago, Neville had become Margaret's guardian. To say he had been unprepared for the gravity of his role would have been a vast understatement. Margaret made trouble wherever she went. He had no notion of what to do with a twenty-year-old with a penchant for waywardness. His current plan was to do everything he could to keep her from eloping with a scoundrel—or being compromised by one.

"Modesty is dreadfully boring, I'm afraid," Lady Charity told him breezily, still squeezing water from her golden plait. "I'd rather be able to splash about in the lake whenever I choose. It's so much more fun."

"Fun," he repeated.

"An amusement," she said, a teasing grin on her lips. "A diversion."

"I'm aware of the word's definition," he bit out, trying not to stare at the round fullness of her breasts straining against her chemise and failing utterly.

He should go. Leave her here to dress. Pretend it had never happened. That he'd never seen the pink points of her hard nipples poking through her chemise like a taunt for his mouth. And yet his feet refused to cooperate. He remained, as if he were one of the nearby trees and had grown roots.

"You seemed unfamiliar with it." Her smile grew. "I thought perhaps I could enlighten you."

She was teasing him. Not just teasing. *Flirting.* She released her braid, and her hands moved to her chemise, grasping the wet fabric.

Surely she didn't intend to remove it.

His neck went hot. "Stop at once, madam."

She didn't. The hem of her chemise lifted, revealing her calves, then her knees. By God. She was going to take it off entirely. He didn't want her to do so. And yet he also very badly did.

But then she paused, gathering the skirt of her undergarment, twisting it, and wringing it out the same way she had her hair.

He could breathe again, but his cock was hard and insistent in his trousers. Inconvenient desire burned through him. Desire he had no business feeling for the maddening Lady Charity Manners.

"What did you think I was going to do?" she asked him with a conspiratorial air. "Take it off?"

Yes, he had. Because he was having thoughts he distinctly should not be having for this outrageous hoyden. He had to think of Margaret, for heaven's sake. Her reputation would suffer should he cause any sort of scandal.

And after losing both her parents, Margaret deserved happiness. She deserved a fine husband, one she'd never find if Neville surrendered to his base instincts and kissed a nearly nude Lady Charity Manners. Because he wouldn't want to stop at kissing.

More warmth crawled up his neck, his ears going hot.

"What part of England has the most dogs?" he blurted.

Oh, lovely. Apparently, he was reverting to his habit of telling dreadful jokes whenever the nervousness that inevitably seized him returned.

4

Lady Charity's brow furrowed. "I have no notion why you've just asked me that, my lord."

She continued wringing out her chemise, pulling it a bit higher and revealing a swath of thigh that would haunt him in his dreams tonight.

"To distract myself," he muttered.

"From what?"

"From your unfortunate state of *dishabille*, Lady Charity," Neville clarified rigidly.

"Oh." Her full lips curved into a sensual smile. "I suppose I've shocked you, but how else was I meant to swim? A lady could drown, bogged down by so many layers. And wouldn't it be positively horrid for me to be unmannerly enough to perish at the Duke and Duchess of Bradford's country house party? So you see, wearing only my chemise for my dip in the lake was actually quite practical of me."

He didn't see anything practical about her transparent chemise or the shadow between her thighs or the way her undergarment clung to her, lovingly revealing her lush figure.

"Bark-shire," he answered for her instead of responding to her ridiculous claim. "Instead of *Berkshire*. The part of England with the most dogs, that is."

Lady Charity stared at him.

"It's a pun," he added faintly.

"I'm aware," she said dryly, echoing his earlier words.

He winced. This was why he loathed polite society. Why he had always eschewed large gatherings until Margaret's period of mourning had ended and he'd been forced to reemerge from his haven in the countryside. Why he dreaded every moment he had to spend in polite conversation. Because he was horrible at it. His brother, Wentworth, had been the garrulous and silver-tongued charmer. He'd been at his best when surrounded by others. Neville, meanwhile, had been content to keep to himself. To keep from humiliating himself just as he was doing now before this stunning, brazen woman.

"You ought to dress before someone else comes along on the path," he forced out. "You'll cause a scandal."

She laughed, the sound mellifluous. "No one would be surprised if the disgraceful Lady Charity Manners caused another scandal. Surely my reputation precedes me."

Was there a hint of bitterness in her voice? Neville thought so.

As if she had all the time in the world to dress, she reached for a petticoat lying atop the pile.

"I don't indulge in frivolous gossip," he told her politely rather than admit that he was indeed aware of the rumors concerning her.

Perhaps worse, that he believed them.

She gave him a searching look, shaking out her petticoat. "Since you're here, you may as well help me."

Help her? That would require proximity.

His denial was swift. "It would be unseemly."

A soft chuckle fell from her lips. "More unseemly than standing here conversing while I'm in my shift? I think not. Come closer, won't you? My bodice has a rather frustrating line of buttons on the back, and I had to twist and contort myself to open them."

She made everything sound practical. As if it were a matter of course that he help her dress. As if it were perfectly ordinary for an unwed lady—or any lady, for that matter—to go about swimming in a lake, nearly nude. What a peculiar woman she was. He found himself annoyingly intrigued.

And moving closer. Damn it, what was this effect she had on him? "Very well," he allowed with great reluctance. "I'll help."

"I promise I won't bite," she teased.

An astonishing thought—he wouldn't mind if she did. But that was all wrong. *She* was all wrong. And he had a niece to squire about. A need to make certain he never made a misstep for Margaret's sake. His family history was already notorious enough. Gamblers, dissolute rakehells, and madmen abounded in the Astley family annals. The title was centuries old, but it was also steeped in disgrace. When Wentworth had died, Neville had taken on the mantle and all the responsibility and tarnish it possessed with the greatest of reluctance.

He cleared his throat. "Let us get this business concluded, Lady Charity."

"For a man who enjoys jokes, you're remarkably lacking in mirth," she observed.

But that was the trouble. He didn't enjoy jokes any more than he enjoyed people. His beleaguered mind had no control over them.

He chose not to respond to her dig.

"Turn," he said instead, taking command of the situation and plucking the petticoat from her hands.

For the sooner he helped her to dress, the sooner he could leave her maddening presence. The sooner he could be far from her side, no longer spurred by the impulse to touch her.

Clearly, he had been celibate for far too long. That was the only reason he couldn't seem to stifle the inconvenient lust roaring through him. Because that was what it was and nothing more.

To his surprise, Lady Charity didn't offer any argument. Instead, she complied, presenting him with her back. For a moment, his greedy gaze devoured her, from the soft skin at her nape where tendrils of golden hair had curled free of their braid, to the nip of her waist and the swell of her rump. He longed to step into her, to wrap his arms around

7

her waist and bury his face in the side of her throat, to breathe in the scent of woman and summer and cool, clear water.

But then he regained his senses and dropped the petticoat over her head, pulling it down and arranging it over her damp chemise. He found the tapes and button and secured it.

"No bustle?" he asked, taking note of the meager pile of garments remaining in the grass.

"Too cumbersome," she said. "Besides, have you any notion how long it takes for them to dry when they've become wet?"

She gave a delicate shudder.

He bent and retrieved her skirt, which was a deep and vibrant shade of purple, but otherwise markedly unornamented and simple. "You do this sort of thing frequently, then?"

"Swimming or disrobing?" she asked cheekily.

"Swimming," he answered curtly, before bringing the skirt over her head as well.

She emerged from the opening in the skirt and cast a look at him over her shoulder. "Whenever I have the chance. There's nothing more delightful than being free in the water. What of you? Do you help a lady dress frequently?"

"Only when I find a mermaid washed ashore and in need of assistance," he quipped, focusing his attentions on the fall of her skirt, making certain it covered her petticoat.

Trying to keep himself from blurting another bloody pun.

Her fingers grazed his as she smoothed a wrinkle from the fabric, and a jolt went through him at the contact. "I shall consider myself fortunate then that you have an affinity for mermaids."

He bent again, retrieving her bodice, realizing belatedly just how many undergarments were missing from her collection. "No corset either?"

"When sneaking out for a swim, it's rather imperative that one wear as few undergarments as possible."

Again, she made her actions sound so perversely practical. And yet they filled him with the fire of a blazing sun. What must it be like to be so carefree and reckless? How he wished he knew. He held the bodice out for her, averting his gaze to keep from availing himself of another view of her pebbled nipples. She stuffed her arms into the sleeves, and he moved to her back and the line of buttons awaiting him.

"Spoken like a lady of experience," he murmured at last, wondering just how often she sneaked about, swimming in lakes.

She stiffened, her spine straightening. "That's what the gossips say about me, isn't it?"

Her voice was brash and bold as ever, but he detected an edge to her words.

"I wouldn't know," he said calmly. "What is a horse's favorite interjection?"

"I haven't an inkling."

He finished the last button. "Hey."

Blast. He couldn't seem to hold his tongue. But he hated the notion that he might have inadvertently paid her insult. He had been speaking of her swimming experience, not her *other* experience. The latter was hardly any concern of his. Neville stepped away from her, even though he longed to remain.

"Thank you for your aid, my lord," she said coolly, whirling about in a swirl of purple and gold, her wet braid flipping over her shoulder. "I promise I won't intrude on your walk tomorrow morning."

There it was again, the suggestion that she knew his morning routine.

"How do you know about my morning walks?" he asked, curious.

"I make it a habit to study the routines of others," she answered. "That way, I can be assured I won't have an interruption when I want to swim."

As he had done this morning. He suddenly felt like a cad.

"It was hardly my intention to do so," he pointed out, belatedly realizing that she hadn't any shoes. "Did you wander this far from the main house in your bare feet?"

"Of course. I dislike walking in wet shoes."

He frowned. "You'll injure yourself."

"Your concern for my welfare is touching, Lord Wilton, but misplaced. I assure you, I can tend to my own feet perfectly well."

The woman was a menace. He'd never met anyone like her. A strange, protective surge overwhelmed him. Neville couldn't shake the feeling that her boldness hid a deep vulnerability. One he recognized, for he shared it.

"I'm certain you can," he offered politely. "Just as I'm sure you know how reckless it is to wander about alone, swimming in nothing more than a chemise, despite the earliness of the hour."

She raised a brow. "Are you chastising me?"

Yes, he reckoned he was. But he could see it would be a mistake to admit it. Lady Charity's pride wouldn't allow such a thing.

"I wouldn't dream of it." He forced a smile and offered her a bow. "I suppose I should take my leave."

Without waiting for her response, he stepped around her and continued on the path, determined to put as much distance between himself and the tempting Lady Charity as possible.

"Wait," she called after him, so softly that he almost didn't hear it.

But he did, and he paused, turning back to her.

She was standing where he'd left her, her damp braid still

draped over her shoulder, bare toes peeping from beneath her hems, so astoundingly lovely that his breath caught. So decidedly improper.

"Thank you, my lord," she said quietly, all the coquettishness and teasing noticeably absent from her voice.

"My pleasure, Lady Charity," he managed past the lump in his throat.

And then he turned again and made haste in his retreat.

CHAPTER 2

⁓

Charity winced as she plucked the thorn from the ball of her foot.

Lord Wilton had been right, curse him. She *had* injured herself. It had happened when she'd taken a shortcut through the rose garden on her return to the manor house. The pain had been instant and intense. She'd been forced to hobble the rest of her way to her chamber before she could finally twist herself into a position where she could find and remove the blasted thing.

She likely should have worn shoes for her hasty visit to the lake that morning. She also probably shouldn't have ventured to the lake for a swim at all. A proper lady certainly wouldn't have dreamed of doing so. But the lovely thing about already having lost one's reputation was that such matters no longer possessed the weight they once had.

When Ainsley had thrown her over in the wake of the Venus painting scandal, he had proven her fall from grace complete. He had also dashed her heart to tiny, unmendable pieces. But that was another matter entirely, and she had shed her last tear over the man she'd once loved. She wouldn't waste another drop on him.

No, indeed. Charity had sworn off men and love forever.

She was perfectly happy as she was. Happier than she would have been as the wife of a man so lacking in faith that he had abandoned her in her darkest hour as if she were a common trollop. But then, that was what the gossips whispered about her. She had sat nude for the famed Richards painting, *Venus at Her Bath*. And that meant she must have allowed Peter Richards into her bed. That she wasn't chaste. That she had seduced not just Peter, but a host of other gentlemen as well.

The rumors had been bad enough.

But what had truly hurt had been the fact that Ainsley had believed them. That he hadn't wanted anything to do with her. How cold and remote he had been the day he had called upon her last. To tell her he couldn't countenance a connection to a woman who was so soiled in the eyes of society.

Soiled.

Rather like her feet were now, stained green and brown from her ill-fated traipse through the rose garden. Charity rose and poured a generous dose of water into a basin, intent upon cleaning both feet. Using a cloth and a decadently floral bar of Winters soap, she washed away the stubborn evidence of her lack of shoes. If only her reputation had been so easily scrubbed clean.

It hadn't. But no matter. She had learned that when a lady's reputation was ruined, she was free. Free to do whatever she wished without fear of recriminations. She was content with her life. She had her dear friends, the Lady's Suffrage Society, her family, plans for travel on the Continent with Auntie Louise. She had everything she required.

She didn't need anyone. And certainly, she didn't need a

husband. Men weren't to be trusted. Flirted with, dallied with, yes. Trusted? Never again.

Charity was just finishing her ablutions when a knock sounded at her door.

"Come," she called without bothering to ascertain who her unexpected visitor was.

Since arriving in Yorkshire for the Duke and Duchess of Bradford's country house party, Charity had been spending a great deal of time with her dear friends Vivi, the duchess, Lady Clementine Hammond, Lady Edith Smythe, and the American heiresses Miss Lucy and Madeline Chartrand. They all made a habit of stopping by one another's rooms to chat.

The door opened to reveal Miss Madeline Chartrand, looking lovely as ever in a morning gown of pale-blue silk, her dark hair coiled into a Grecian braid with small curls fringing her face.

"Good morning," Madeline greeted cheerfully, breezing over the threshold and closing the door behind her. "You're looking decidedly...damp this fine summer day. Whatever were you doing, my dear?"

"I went for a morning swim," she said, rising and shaking out her skirts. "I've only just returned."

"That would explain it." Madeline nodded as if it were perfectly customary for Charity to have done so, her American sensibilities making her rather less inclined toward censure. "Were you swimming in the river or the lake?"

The River Derwent meandered through the massive Sherborne Manor estate, but it was a much farther walk than the man-made lake. "The lake, of course."

"With the murderous swans?" Madeline seated herself in one of the chairs flanking the hearth. "You're a brave woman."

Charity chuckled, joining her friend in the chair at her

side, for the swans were rather unimpressed by human inter-lopers. "I've charmed them."

"Of course you have. I shouldn't be surprised."

"Where is your sister this morning?" Charity asked, trying not to think of the man who had been the only other presence at the lake that morning.

Viscount Wilton with his stiff bearing, his nonsensical puns, and the face and body of an Adonis. How unsettled she'd felt at her discovery of him, standing there on the bank of the lake near her discarded garments. Unsettled because she found herself drawn to him, even though she knew she shouldn't be. He was the last man in the world she should have found herself not just intrigued by, but attracted to.

"Lucy has found herself in a bit of trouble with the Earl of Rexingham," Madeline said, dispersing Charity's unwanted thoughts. "I do believe she's seeking him out in the hope he won't try to ask our mother for her hand in marriage."

Lucy and the earl? Charity wouldn't have guessed it. But then, they certainly weren't the only ones who had been seeking each other out in secret at this house party. Clementine had found herself in more than one compromising position with the Marquess of Dorset. Lady Edith had been thoroughly wooed by the dashing Mr. Valentine Blakemoor, and now Lucy would perhaps have to wed Rexingham.

"Marriage?" Charity shook her head. "That poor dear."

"Indeed. Lucy isn't particularly pleased, but the earl sounds determined."

"Your mother will be happy at the prospect of a match between the two of them."

It was a well-known fact that the hideously wealthy Mrs. William Chartrand of New York City was determined to secure each of her daughters an aristocratic match. Even if Lucy and Madeline had other ideas about her aspirations.

Madeline sighed. "I expect she will. The moral of this

particular story is that one should never linger in dark gardens with handsome lords."

The Earl of Rexingham was indeed quite attractive. However, it wasn't the earl Charity found herself thinking about yet again. Viscount Wilton was haunting her with the same stubborn persistence with which he had lingered earlier at the lake. She tried not to remember how it had felt to have him stand near, his fingers brushing over hers, his presence at her back burning into her.

"A well-timed reminder," Charity said. "Handsome lords are notoriously untrustworthy."

Or, at least, her handsome lord had been. But then, had Ainsley ever truly been hers? Clearly not. And now, he could go to the devil for all she cared. He hadn't deserved her. He'd done her a favor in showing her the man he truly was before she'd spent an inevitable lifetime of misery at his side.

"*All* handsome men are," Madeline said grimly. "The ones with the fair faces always seem to have the hearts of stone."

There was a tale in her friend's words, but Charity didn't want to pry. No one knew better than she did just how painful it could be to have to relive the past and all the hurts it contained. Far more painful than a mere thorn in the foot.

Charity sighed. "Truer words have never been spoken, dear. I often think about how vastly unfair it is—the standards we as women are held to versus the standards of men. A man can have a dreadful reputation, and he's a sought-after rake. But when a woman has one, she's ruined."

Ainsley had been no different. He'd been a celebrated and well-known rake. But he had pursued Charity, charming her, convincing her that he was reformed. That he loved her. She'd given her heart to him despite the rumors of his many past conquests. But when the rumor about *Venus at Her Bath* had surfaced, he'd been swift to judge her. To deem her unsuitable.

"And to be denied the right to vote when the laws that are made affect us," Madeline added. "It's unconscionable, both at home in New York City and here, in England. Something must be done."

"We're certainly trying to do something," Charity said. "Even if it feels as if we never get anywhere."

"Trying is the most important thing," Madeline agreed. "We must never surrender."

"May we remain strong in our determination to fight, even after some of us are married," Charity added, giving voice to the concern that had been troubling her.

With so many of her friends about to marry, she couldn't help but wonder if they would be as steadfast in their support of the Lady's Suffrage Society. But of course, all the leading and most influential members of the society were already married, so perhaps there was hope. Not all husbands were disapproving autocrats like Ainsley would have been.

"It feels as if this has been the summer of so much change," her friend said thoughtfully. "Or perhaps it's merely been this house party that has been the cause of it."

"It certainly seems to have made an impact on some more than others," Charity agreed. "Thankfully, I'm exempt from the lures of rakes and rogues. I'm happy to remain as I am, no one to break my heart or otherwise disappoint me."

"Agreed, my friend," Madeline said, rising again. "I suppose I should leave you to dress for breakfast. Will I see you downstairs?"

"I'll be there," Charity confirmed, getting to her feet as well. "Just as soon as I can change out of my damp clothes and into something that won't shock our fellow guests."

Although, in truth, if she did shock anyone, Charity didn't truly care. Let the tongues wag. She was unapologetically herself. And she liked who she was, even if other members of society looked down their noses at her and gossiped. Thank heavens for her friends.

But for a reason she couldn't explain and refused to examine, as Charity saw Madeline to the door and turned her mind to dressing for the morning, she couldn't seem to shake the memory of Viscount Wilton's gaze as it had traveled over her form by the lake, nor the unsettling way his proximity had made her feel. It hardly mattered. All men were the same, and the proper lord had made his disapproval of her morning swim more than apparent.

Viscount Wilton, like the Earl of Ainsley, could trot off into the sunset for all she cared, never to return.

~

NEVILLE COULDN'T FIND MARGARET.

It was the very devil of a predicament. If he'd been a woman, he could have gone into her chamber when she failed to appear at breakfast. He might have conferred with the other ladies in attendance. He would have known what to do or, at the very least, had some manner of addressing his concerns.

But he was a man.

A great, stupid, awkward lout who didn't know the slightest thing about women in general outside the bedchamber and most certainly not how to look after a wayward, stubborn twenty-year-old niece.

And so he found himself pacing about the great hall of Sherborne Manor without an inkling as to what action he might take next. Margaret often found herself in scrapes. But she had never failed to appear for breakfast. Not before, anyway. What could have happened? Had one of the gentlemen compromised her? Seduced her? Otherwise lured her away?

By God, if something untoward had happened to her, he would never forgive himself.

Frustrated, he paced some more. Paced until he was dizzied with a combination of movement and sickening worry and fear. Just when he decided he would have to seek out his hostess and beg her assistance, the sound of feminine laughter echoing off the marble reached him.

Familiar laughter.

He spun about in time to see Margaret sweeping across the hall. Relief hit him along with another emotion, because *she* was at Margaret's side, laughing with her conspiratorially. The morning lake's presiding Venus. Scandal waiting to happen. A scandal that had *already* happened.

Lady Charity Manners.

Neville strode toward them, anger rising like a swelling tide. "Margaret, where were you at breakfast?"

Belatedly recalling his manners, he offered a perfunctory bow. Lady Charity had something to do with this. He would wager everything he owned that wasn't entailed. A great deal, as it happened. He might not have been born the heir, but he had turned his sharp mind to amassing a fortune by making shrewd investments. He might never have been adept at socializing, but he had a keen head for business, and it had not disappointed him.

"I haven't breakfasted just yet, Uncle," Margaret said, smiling with innocent cheer. "Lady Charity and I crossed paths in the garden, and we had the most delightful conversation about traveling on the Continent."

Neville spared a glance for the vexing lady in question, who looked the picture of elegance and refinement in a promenade gown of navy silk ornamented with pink wild roses and a hint of blonde lace on the cuffs and bodice. Her hair had been swept into a formal chignon, with curls left to feather over her high forehead. Her full, sensual lips were tilted upward at the corners, as if she were attempting to subdue a taunting smile.

He had never in his life wanted to simultaneously kiss a woman and deliver a searing setdown. But he did now.

"I was worried," he told Margaret shortly. "You might have sent a note."

"Forgive me," his niece said. "It wasn't my intention to cause you to fret. I had no notion of how much time had passed. Lady Charity was telling me all about the plans she has to visit Paris with her aunt. She invited me to accompany them."

"Absolutely not," he bit out.

His niece would gallivant in France with a hoyden like Lady Charity Manners over his dead body.

"But, Uncle," Margaret began, her expression turning stubborn.

It was a look he recognized, for he had seen it often enough on his brother's face. The memory of Wentworth, still so fresh despite the year since his death, made Neville's heart clench painfully. He forced the thought aside, lest he do something more humiliating than blurting puns, like turn into a watering pot.

"I'm afraid I'm unbending on the matter," he said quickly before she could offer further protestations. "As your guardian, it would be remiss of me to allow you to travel abroad unaccompanied."

"But I would be accompanied by Lady Charity and her aunt," his niece protested, apparently blithely unaware of Neville's reasons for refusal.

He cleared his throat, awkwardness seizing him. "No, Margaret."

While he strove for a gentle tone, the words still emerged sharp and clipped. Although he tried to avert his gaze from Lady Charity, he saw her flinch out of the corner of his eye.

Something akin to guilt speared him, but he tamped it down. He was all Margaret had in this world. He was her protector. She'd lost her parents. He was a poor replacement, but he was doing his utmost. And that meant that he couldn't allow her to gad about with a reckless companion who would only serve to ruin her reputation.

"Perhaps you could mull it over," Margaret suggested hopefully. "Female companionship would do wonders for me, Uncle. You've said yourself often enough that you wish you could provide me with it."

Yes, he had. And he was very seriously considering finding a wife. He *would* find one. Someone who would be nothing at all like Lady Charity Manners. Someone who would never dream of swimming nearly naked in a lake at a house party with dozens of other guests milling about to catch her. Someone who wouldn't sit nude for a painting that then was put on display before London. Someone who didn't relish being scandalous the way most ladies prided themselves on being respectable.

Someone who followed the rules.

That was who he would find.

And that wasn't the golden-haired Siren at Margaret's side.

"The answer is and will remain no, my dear," he informed his niece, gentling his tone. "It wouldn't be proper."

"I think what your uncle is trying to say is that *I'm* not proper," Lady Charity said then. "And he isn't wrong, Margaret. I pride myself on being who I am, as I am."

His eyes strayed to her against his will. And despite himself, he drank in the sight for the second time, finding details he'd missed the first. The long lashes, her retroussé nose, a hint of golden freckles lining the bridge in a sign she often eschewed hats outdoors. Because of course she did.

"I was saying nothing of the kind, my lady," he denied.

"I'm responsible for my niece. It's my duty to see her well and happily settled here in England. Dashing to the Continent for a frivolous journey will hardly accomplish that goal, which my brother clearly stated for her."

"I suppose it never occurred to you that she might not want to find herself settled with a husband," Lady Charity said archly. "Nor that perhaps Margaret's own aspirations for herself might differ from those her father decreed for her."

No, it hadn't. But he refused to bend on the matter. He wouldn't argue with a lunatic who walked barefoot and swam with fishes and swans and thwarted every proper stricture of society as if it were a tedious bore.

He cleared his throat. "I'm doing what my brother asked of me, Lady Charity. Now, if you'll excuse us, I do believe I'll escort my niece to a late breakfast."

"I don't want breakfast," Margaret said mulishly. "I'll take a tray in my room."

He heard the petulance of a child stomping her foot.

Neville sighed. "Margaret, please don't be stubborn on this matter. I'm only doing what is best for you, as I always have."

"What is best for me according to *you*," his niece countered pointedly. "I shall see you later, Uncle. For now, I find myself in need of a restorative nap."

Before he could further protest, Margaret flounced away in a swirl of agitated silk. Saints preserve him from meddling females. He watched her go, feeling that same abysmal sense of failure that had been dwelling in his gut from the moment he'd first taken on the weighty responsibility of not just his brother's title, but his daughter as well.

"You might as well have said the truth," Lady Charity said.

Reluctantly, he looked to her, trying to erase the memory of her pointed pink nipples under her wet chemise from that morning. But it was no use. It was indelibly burned upon his mind.

"I did say the truth, madam," he said tightly.

"The truth is that I'm too scandalous for you to consider allowing your niece to linger in my presence," she continued quite as if he hadn't protested. "Admit it."

Conceding that she was correct would hardly further his cause.

"You seem determined to have an argument this morning, my lady," he said instead. "But I find I haven't the patience for contention. I've spent the last hour wondering where my niece was, fearing the worst."

"And discovering it to be true, no doubt," she quipped tartly, her sensual lips tightening, the earlier traces of a smile decidedly gone.

He had displeased her. For some reason, that nettled him. There was something about this woman that called to him in a way he'd never experienced before. He prided himself on his control, his restraint. He didn't need to give in to base urges like some men. He didn't keep a mistress or visit brothels. The lovers he'd known had been few. Dearth of female companionship was one downfall of becoming a recluse.

Perhaps it was the length of time since he'd last known a lover was the reason for this infernal reaction to her. This need to assuage her concerns.

"You are hardly the worst I feared, my lady."

She raised a brow. "You needn't lie on my account. Now, if you'll excuse me, I've more important matters to attend."

Something in her countenance, in her voice, gave her away. She may well have acted as if nothing concerned her, but she was not nearly as unaffected as she pretended. The edge in her voice earlier when he'd seen her at the lake returned to him.

"Wait," he said. "I'll accompany you."

Her eyes narrowed and her lips pursed. "You haven't asked where I'm going or what I'll be doing."

"It doesn't matter."

She was staring at him with blatant suspicion. For a moment, he feared she would refuse him, and he wasn't even certain why her doing so would bother him. And yet it did.

"Come along, then," she said cheerfully.

The sudden merriment in her voice was Neville's first cause for concern.

The second was the fact that she didn't wait for him to offer his arm. Nor did she walk with him. Instead, she sailed forward, with him following in her wake like a dinghy after a grand yacht.

CHAPTER 3

*B*oating."

Charity didn't miss the dismay coloring Viscount Wilton's pleasantly deep voice.

"Of course." She gave him her brightest smile, hoping he would see the lack of wisdom in insisting upon accompanying her now and go.

She already knew he couldn't swim; he'd revealed as much when the Marquess of Dorset had saved an orange kitten floating downstream in the River Derwent during the house party.

"What is a fishing rod's favorite dance?" he asked abruptly.

Another pun? She was beginning to suspect the viscount blurted them whenever he was nervous. It was a habit as singular as it was endearing. Not that she found him so. She was impervious to masculine charms.

Charity thought for a moment, deciding to humor him. "A reel?"

"Indeed." He wasn't smiling.

He looked almost funereal.

"Tell me, do you object to all forms of amusement, my lord?" she couldn't resist asking.

They stood together in the cool shade of the boathouse, the sun beckoning them beyond, a handful of small wooden boats at the ready.

He frowned. "Hardly."

His lips were distracting. She wondered briefly what they would feel like on hers, and then she soundly trounced that curiosity right out of her mind. He was the last man she wanted to kiss.

"You disapprove of swimming," she pointed out.

"Unaccompanied and in an improper state of *dishabille*, yes."

"You disapprove of travel."

"Not travel, in particular. Although there's nothing quite as lovely and familiar and comforting as one's home."

She knew him to be a man who eschewed society. Until this house party, they'd never crossed paths. But then, he had also inherited fairly recently. His period of mourning must have only just ended. His words made sense to her. And she could understand the sentiment, even if she'd never felt particularly at home in either her father's country estate or his grand town house.

"Travel with *me*," she reminded him, unable to keep the bitterness from her voice.

Yes, it had rankled that he had so hastily and unequivocally denied his niece's desire for adventure. The younger woman was quite kindhearted. She'd lost her parents in a carriage accident and had been left adrift in the world, no other close relatives, save the viscount.

"I have a duty to my niece," he said coolly. "My brother wanted to see her settled. She wouldn't be settled in Paris."

"Perhaps she doesn't wish to be settled," Charity pointed

out. "Have you considered that, my lord? Not every woman wishes to marry and find herself turned into a broodmare."

"Are you speaking of Margaret or yourself, Lady Charity?" he asked shrewdly.

And curse the man. For once, she was at a loss for words, in danger of blurting something foolish. What was it about him that affected her so? Surely it wasn't his handsome face. She'd always favored tall men with blond hair, but pale-green eyes weren't ordinarily her preference. His, now that she thought upon it, were rather unusual. Unlike any she'd seen before.

"Do you want to get in the boat or not?" she asked, irritated with him for seeing her too clearly.

For coming too close to the truth when they'd scarcely done more than exchange banter and small talk before this morning.

He cocked his head, those interesting eyes searing her. "I've been charged with seeing to her future, and I assure you that means I'll take Margaret's wishes into consideration. I'm hardly an ogre."

His tone had gentled from one of irritation to earnest explanation.

"I didn't call you an ogre," she said grudgingly.

"No, you merely thought me one."

They stared at each other, at an impasse.

Charity heaved a sigh, immensely annoyed now because she was beginning to like Viscount Wilton, and that simply wasn't acceptable. "I'm getting into the boat, with or without you. I can row myself just as well."

"Yes, but you'll be alone."

He seemed to be speaking of more than the boat. Perhaps a thinly veiled reminder that a woman ought to seek a future as a wife instead of remaining free to do as she wished.

"And there won't be anyone to vex me, will there?" she asked triumphantly, stepping into one of the nearest boats.

To her dismay, she hadn't been quite prepared for the give of the vessel under her when she stepped off the sturdy dock. The boat swayed on the water, and her stupid, cumbersome gown, complete with bustle, was of no aid. It made her reaction slow, sending her listing to the side like a ship about to capsize. A wild moment of panic shot through her as she failed to regain her balance, the rocking boat and her heavy undergarments uniting to send her toward the waiting water.

An unladylike squeal left her, her arms flailing for purchase as it all happened at once.

But then, just as suddenly, strong hands were on her waist, steadying her. Drawing her into a well-muscled, lean, masculine frame. His arms banded around her, protective and strong, and that was when she realized he was in the boat with her. She clung to him as the boat swayed and rocked, water splashing off the sides, her cheek pressed to his hard chest as her heart pounded furiously. He smelled of lemon and musk with a hint of forest, and for some reason, she inhaled deeply, burrowing her nose in the fabric of his shirt, just above the vee of his tweed waistcoat.

He had saved her from falling into the lake.

A man who couldn't swim. Weighed down by her layers of proper undergarments and her walking boots, by her silk and cotton and boning and padding, even someone as skilled at swimming as Charity was might well have drowned.

She swallowed, her arms still wrapped around him, and made a shocking realization. It felt good being held by this man. Astonishingly good. And she didn't ever want him to let her go.

"Steady, Lady Charity," he said, his voice gruff and thick, a rumble against her ear.

And how ridiculous it seemed, for him to observe formality when she was wrapped around him like an ivy vine. She ought to release him. And she would. In a moment. But she couldn't. Her arms were locked, and his divine scent was still invading her senses.

"Thank you," she managed.

"You're welcome." His hands, pressed tightly to her back, moved.

They glided slowly, reassuringly, along her spine. And somehow that simple touch, through all her layers—the feeling of his hands, which were surprisingly large—made her entirely too aware of him in a new way.

Aware of not just his handsomeness and strength and scent. But of him as a man. And, more troubling, of herself as a woman. It made her feel flushed all over, despite the coolness of the shaded brick boathouse. Caused a languorous pull of something dark and dangerous to glide through her. Something she hadn't allowed herself to feel at all in a very long time.

"Do you have your balance?" he asked stiffly, quite shattering the feelings blossoming inside her.

Just as well. They were feelings she had no business entertaining.

"I think so." She made the mistake of tilting her head back and looking up at him then.

They were still pressed flush against each other. And he was looking down at her with concern. But not just concern. Something else. Something she recognized because she'd seen it before.

Masculine interest.

His gaze dipped to her lips, and she licked them instinctively, a new feeling chasing all the rest. It crashed over her, sudden and forceful and undeniable.

Desire.

Good heavens, she wanted the proper, formal, disapproving Viscount Wilton's mouth on hers. She wanted him to kiss her.

"Excellent," he said, setting her away, rather as if she'd caught flame and he feared he would get burned if she lingered too near to him.

The haste of his action made the small boat tilt and tip to the side again, but this time, she was prepared, and she planted her feet in the hull.

He reached for her once more, his hands back on her waist, a flush stealing along his cheekbones as he stepped into her until they were breast to chest. "I'm sorry. I'm afraid I haven't sea legs."

"This lake is hardly the sea," she couldn't help but tease.

She didn't know where the attempt at levity emerged from. Perhaps her own awkwardness. And how strange and alarming that was, for she'd never felt a lack of confidence. Not even after Ainsley had thrown her over and left her devastated. Lady Charity Manners kept her head held high.

But there was no denying it. She felt different when he pressed her tightly against him. Different with his pale eyes glittering into hers in the shadows. She felt uncertain of herself and yet also so very potently alive.

Yes, that was the word for it. *Alive.*

"No, of course it isn't," he agreed, unsmiling.

She couldn't decide if he feared any sudden movement might send her overboard or if he feared the water itself.

"You can release me now," she told him gently.

For as much as she enjoyed this closeness—relished it, even—she didn't dare allow herself to like it too much. One broken heart was enough to last a lifetime, and she knew all too well that she was the last sort of woman a polite, strict man like the viscount would ever want.

Not that it mattered. Marriage was out of the question

for Charity. Once, she had dreamed of becoming a wife and mother. But that dream had swiftly been obliterated by the cold, unsmiling man she loved telling her he required a wife who was above reproach, untarnished and untouched by scandal. Someone who, quite specifically, wasn't her.

"Release you," Wilton repeated, swallowing hard.

In fascination, she watched the dip of his Adam's apple above his neckcloth. It wasn't too pronounced as some gentlemen's were, but it was, rather, like the rest of his appearance, disturbingly attractive. For a foolish moment, she thought about burying her face in his neck, pressing her lips to his skin.

"Yes, my lord. It ought to be a simple process, really. Move first your left hand and then your right. Or your right hand first, followed by the left. The preference is yours. If you're feeling particularly adventurous, you might remove them both at once."

He blinked, and it was as if a mask had come over his expression. The heat and vulnerability simmering in his eyes vanished behind a window of civility. "Of course. Why did the fisherman throw back his catch?"

Oh dear. Something was certainly amiss. Her vanity would have adored to know that Viscount Wilton was so strongly attracted to her despite her many faults that he simply couldn't let her go. But his sudden pun suggested distinctly otherwise.

He was nervous.

"I'm afraid I don't know," she said, trying not to notice the faint glistening prickles of whiskers on his angular jaw.

Nor to think about how those bristles might feel against her lips.

"Because it smelt."

She bit her lip, because the pun was so terrible it was almost comical. But she wasn't sure she should laugh just now. Would she be laughing with him, or at him? Lord Wilton's expression was quite severe. It looked as if it might have been cut from stone.

"You're afraid of water," she guessed.

His lips tightened, a muscle working in his jaw. "I'm... uncomfortable with it."

"Why?" she asked softly, needing to know for some inexplicable reason.

Wanting some small part of this man that would be hers. Even if it was all she dared to claim.

He inhaled sharply, his expression pained. "When I was a lad, my younger brother drowned. His nurse was drunk and she fell asleep, and Christopher wandered into the pond at our family seat in Wiltshire."

Anguish made her heart seize. "I'm so very sorry, my lord."

"If the rest of us, the domestics, anyone had been watching... But it happened so quickly. My father had it drained immediately. It was too late."

The barely leashed pain in his voice wound itself around her heart, squeezing.

"I'm sorry," she repeated. "I never would have asked you to go boating with me had I known."

"Of course you wouldn't, and it's been many years since the incident. Five-and-twenty, in fact. I was just a lad of six at the time. I had hoped by now that being on the water would no longer affect me."

He gave her a tight smile that told her it did.

"Let's get out of the boat, shall we?" she invited.

He gave a terse nod. "You first, my lady. I'll help you."

She wanted to protest that she didn't need his assistance. That she could see to herself as always. But then she recalled how she'd nearly splashed into the lake upon her descent into the boat. And she sensed how much it had cost him to rush to her rescue. To stand here with her now and offer to assist her out first.

And she accepted his offer. "Thank you."

With an ease and a quickness that left her breathless, he lifted her by the waist, settling her back on the dock, taking care to make certain she had her footing before letting go. Grasping one of the wooden mooring poles, he pulled himself from the boat as well.

Suddenly, they were standing face-to-face, their footing sure on the wooden planks of the boathouse dock. Viscount Wilton stared down at her, solemn and stern and forbidding. Longing crashed into her. A need to feel those lips on hers, to wrap her arms around him, to offer him comfort. To give and to take in return.

In the wake of Ainsley's defection, she'd been initially shattered, and then after the worst of the shock and pain had turned her numb, she'd decided to prove him right. She'd kissed a string of gentlemen in revenge. But never had she felt this strange, burning need inside her that she felt now. Not for any of them.

"My lord," she began.

"What does—" he started simultaneously and then stopped.

There was no mistaking the nervousness in his voice, nor the rigidity in his broad shoulders. He'd been about to make another pun.

"You go first, my lady," he said solicitously.

She studied his severe countenance. "Do I make you nervous, my lord?"

His mouth tightened. "Of course not."

Perhaps it was the proximity of the water.

"Good," she said, taking one of his hands in hers and linking their fingers. "Then come along with me."

She tugged him from the boathouse without awaiting

permission. And he went with her, a silent, strong, mysterious presence.

This was going to lead to trouble, she had no doubt.

～

HE HAD to think of Margaret.

To think of the potential scandal he could unleash. He was already the source of hideous gossip, and he knew it. One of the mad Astleys, they said. Because he didn't prefer London or the social whirl. Because he'd always hidden himself away where he'd felt more comfortable. And what would they say now, if they were to see him being led about by Lady Charity Manners, the most outrageous hoyden still reluctantly accepted in polite society?

It would be disastrous for Margaret's chances to make a good match and find happiness.

He had to get away from Lady Charity. To go back to the manor house and forget how fetching she'd looked in the cool shade of the boathouse, every bit as lovely and tempting as she had been wearing perilously little and dripping with lake water that morning. But there was something about her that drew him to her, as if she were a magnet and he a hapless piece of metal.

He wanted to be near her. As close to her as possible. Her fingers were laced through his, and she was pulling him unceremoniously down a path. He felt rather like a dilapidated sulky being tugged along by a sleek racehorse.

"Where are you taking me, my lady?" he asked wryly.

She cast a glance over her shoulder, the coquette once again firmly in place. "You'll see."

Her blue eyes sparkled with mischief, and the heavy weight of the past that had settled over him in the boathouse lifted. There was something about Lady Charity Manners that was intoxicating. Something about her lack of decorum that was infectious. She made him want to do wild and reckless things. She made him want to kiss her.

And more.

But he mustn't think of that now.

Or ever.

She led him past one of the swans so notorious for guarding the lake. The devils had bitten any number of houseguests and otherwise menaced them. Thus far, he'd managed to escape unscathed. The bird raised its head at their approach.

"Not now, Honoré," Lady Charity chided. "Go back to sleep, my fine fellow."

And to Neville's astonishment, the swan gave its brilliant white wings a flap and settled back down, as if obeying her command. They passed by, the swan blinking at them but otherwise remaining immobile.

"Have you bewitched the bird, madam?" he couldn't help but ask, wondering if she had not also bewitched him.

It would certainly seem she had. Why else would he submit to being pulled down a path by this unapologetic minx, when every sound, reasonable, practical, responsible part of him knew he ought to be running in the opposite direction?

"We've made friends." She cast another look over her shoulder, a grin on her lips that he wanted to feel against his. "No dawdling, my lord, or he may well change his mind and decide he wants to have you for his luncheon."

He chuckled. "I think I'm a bit too large to make a meal for a swan."

"Honoré fancies himself a dragon, however. I'd still keep your distance from him, were I you. He doesn't like most people."

"Only you," Neville said quietly.

Thoughtfully.

"I may be an appalling disgrace to society, but my swan friends adore me."

There was that hardness edging her voice again, an undercurrent he didn't miss. Although she made light of her reputation, he would wager it was also a source of contention. Beneath the bold cheer and the vivaciousness of Lady Charity Manners, there lay a darkness. And he wanted to chase it from her. To find whatever it was, lay it bare, heal, and protect her.

It was a strange feeling, particularly in relation to a woman he scarcely knew. One he didn't dare spend much more time with if he was wise. Neville had always prided himself on his intelligence. But he was beginning to wonder at it now.

"Your swan friends," he repeated bemusedly.

Here was the reminder he needed that Lady Charity was, in addition to being wayward and scandalous, quite daft.

"As I said." Another flirtatious smile over her shoulder. "Come, my lord. Are your feet made of lead?"

No, but he was certain that his head was. It was the only explanation for allowing himself to be led deeper into the copse of trees surrounding the man-made lake. Farther from the manor house, where the chances of their being seen dwindled. Where anything was possible.

His cock suddenly leapt to attention at the notion, and the same desire that had been festering inside him since that morning rekindled its flame, burning hot and bright. Good God, he should be appalled with himself.

He was. He would be.

Later.

For now, he was content to follow Lady Charity Manners wherever it was she had decided to take him. Perhaps, of the two of them, he was the daft one.

The cool shade of the trees enveloped them, the scent of the leaves and pungent earth mingling with the sweetness of her perfume. She led him to a wrought-iron bench that had been strategically placed beneath a pair of thick, wizened tree trunks, no doubt for the view of the lake beyond.

"Here we are," she announced. "From here, we can admire the water without needing to be on it. Sit with me, Lord Wilton?"

Warmth trickled through his chest, unexpected and potent. He shouldn't linger with her. His body's reaction was proof of just how dangerous staying in her presence could be.

"How did you know about this spot?" he asked instead of answering her invitation.

He had traveled around the lake on his early-morning walks without ever taking note of the inviting, private seating area.

Lady Charity smiled, and it was the sort of smile that reflected in her eyes. "I'm quite adept at noticing things other people miss."

He wondered if she was speaking of him. But no, that was fanciful. She was only speaking of the bench and its position overlooking the lake.

Neville gestured for her to seat herself first. "A talent indeed, Lady Charity. Perhaps one belonging solely to mermaids."

He waited for her to settle on the bench and then folded his taller frame into the wrought iron at her side, uncomfortably aware of their proximity yet again. Her flowered, blue silk skirts brushed his thigh. Their fingers were still entwined. Belatedly realizing it, he slipped his hand from hers, moving it to a polite distance.

"I'm hardly a mermaid," she said softly, her regard

singeing him. "I'm merely a lady who dislikes anything impinging on her freedom."

What a strange way to view the world. He wasn't sure it explained her lack of concern for propriety. But he supposed it wasn't his duty to discover whether it did.

"I hope you weren't instructing my niece on the finer art of morning lake swims," he said. His entire mind seemed to have deserted him, and he couldn't think of anything better to say beneath the intensity of her stare.

Not even a pun.

"She seems a clever young lady. I daresay she's already discovered the merits of enjoying her own liberty without my influence."

The tart coolness in her tone told him he had inadvertently paid her an insult. Blast. He was going about this all wrong, making her think he disapproved of her. He did disapprove of her morning swim, but not for the reason she likely thought. Initially, perhaps. But her kindness at the boathouse—her calm acceptance and tender understanding —had given him a peek behind the mask she wore.

There was far more to Lady Charity Manners than she allowed the world to see. And suddenly, quite desperately, he wanted to be the one to see it. To find the heart of a woman beating beneath her façade.

The realization shocked him.

Bemused him.

Troubled him.

He cleared his throat. "I wasn't suggesting a lady shouldn't enjoy autonomy, Lady Charity. But surely you must admit the peril of swimming alone in nothing more than your undergarments."

"The only peril to me this morning was from a viscount who seemed to enjoy the sight of me in my undergarments all too well."

Her shrewd observation had heat of a different sort creeping up his neck. The nervousness returned, warring with the desire he felt for her. With the certainty that she could see far more of him than he wished to reveal.

Don't do it, Neville. Don't say another pun. Don't—

"Why is swearing like an old coat?" he blurted, beginning a familiar pun he'd already made use of at this very house party.

He'd been seated beside Lady Edith Smythe at dinner then, and she had guessed the answer, surprising him.

The corners of Lady Charity's lips went up ever so slightly, and unless he was mistaken, her gaze fell to his mouth just for a moment. "Are you trying to distract me with a joke, my lord?"

"A pun."

She tilted her head, considering him. "Is there a difference between the two?"

"A pun is a very specific sort of joke, a play on words. A joke is merely anything that is humorous. Jokes are relatively easy to make. Puns require more thought."

She smiled again, and it was like the sun bursting through thunderclouds. He felt everything he hadn't allowed himself to feel for a brief, stunning few seconds of absolute clarity.

It was terrifying. His heart pounded so hard and fast that he was sure she could hear it.

"Fair enough." Her eyes narrowed, those long, golden lashes sweeping low to partially obscure his view of blue that possessed more vibrant brilliance than any sky he'd ever seen. "Tell me."

He was lost.

Lost in her eyes. In her smile. In her vitality, her heat, her scent of summer rose blossoms and bergamot. In her beauty and recklessness and unexpected kindness. In everything that was her.

And he didn't know what she was expecting him to say. His mind was blanker than a fresh sheet of paper.

"Tell you what?" he asked.

Her lips curved, and good God, when she truly smiled, the effect was devastating. "The answer to your pun, of course. Why is swearing like an old coat?"

Ah, blast and damn. He'd forgotten already.

He swallowed. "Because it's a bad habit."

She chuckled, the sound soft and feminine and delightful. It shouldn't have had a rousing effect on him. Objectively, it was a simple reaction to his pun. Simple amusement, nothing more complex. But his body was beyond his control now, and that husky chuckle made his already thickening cock hard as a rock as he sat there innocently beside her on the bench.

It was unthinkable.

Unforgivable.

"I do believe your puns are improving, Lord Wilton," Lady Charity allowed.

His puns may have been improving, but his restraint and common sense were both in steady decline. As evidenced by the fact that he was sitting here with her on this cursed bench, not just enjoying her company but entranced by her. Wanting so much more of her than he could ever have or dare to ask for.

He had to collect his wits. Likely, it was the shock of finding himself in a boat earlier after over twenty years of abstaining from that particular source of entertainment. It was the fear that had seized him. Perhaps it had temporarily rendered him unable to form proper thoughts.

He cleared his throat. "Thank you, my lady. I've enjoyed our chat. However, I believe we should both return to the main house before we're missed. I'll need to check on my niece."

Her smile faded, and he wished he weren't the source of its retreat. "Of course." She rose, shaking out her skirts demurely, smoothing wrinkles from the voluminous layers. "Forgive me for keeping you too long."

Neville stood, wishing he could stay here with her, beneath the boughs of the trees, before the glistening lake, forever. That he didn't have to return to the swarm of fellow houseguests.

But he couldn't remain, and the charmed, reckless world of a mermaid wasn't where he belonged.

Formally, he proffered his arm. "Allow me to accompany you, my lady."

She glanced down, looking pensive. "I don't think so, my lord. I'll carry on with a bit of a walk. The fresh air, I find, is so improving. Thank you for humoring me for a time."

She turned then and walked in the opposite direction of the manor house. Neville watched her go, rubbing his chest, trying to chase the bereft hollow lodged there. Only when she'd disappeared from view did he retreat to all the duties that awaited him.

The truth of it was, she had been humoring him—and not the other way around.

CHAPTER 4

"It was all incredibly scandalous," Madeline relayed with her signature enthusiasm and flair for the dramatic, her dark eyes sparkling. "Lucy was apparently in *quite* an embrace with the Earl of Rexingham, and the Marchioness of Featherstone walked in upon them and swooned."

Their little coterie—Madeline and Lucy, Vivi, Edith, Charity, and Clementine—had assembled in Vivi's cozy sitting room for an important meeting that had nothing to do with the Lady's Suffrage Society and everything to do with Lucy and the earl.

"It's the second time that woman has swooned this house party alone," Charity pointed out unkindly, unable to keep the bitterness from her voice. "It is a miracle she hasn't run out of hartshorn by now. Or been laid low by a blow to her head. Forgive me for my bluntness, dear Edith."

She harbored no tenderness in her heart for the dowager marchioness. Lady Featherstone and her sharp, gossiping tongue had been responsible for the thorough spread of the rumor concerning *Venus at Her Bath* and Charity. She was the reason Charity had lost Ainsley.

A loss, she reminded herself sternly, that had been a blessing in disguise. Not that she could tell that to her devastated, brokenhearted self. At the time, she'd been sure she would never find any source of comfort or joy again.

"*Maman* likely brought an entire trunk of hartshorn," Lady Edith said, her blue gaze shrewd behind her gold-rimmed spectacles, her flaming-red hair secured in a simple chignon. "She'll never run out of it. Swooning is her favorite pastime aside from gossip."

The dowager marchioness was Lady Edith's mother, which often proved the source of awkwardness amongst the friends in their set. Lady Featherstone's penchant for spreading rumors was every bit as well-known in society as Charity's fall from grace. Fortunately, Edith was more than familiar with her mother's shortcomings. And while, until recently, she'd been content to do her mother's bidding, she had truly emerged from her shell during the house party. Charity was proud of her friend for summoning her courage and having the daring to defy her overbearing mother.

They all were.

"Do we truly need to relive the ignominious events of this morning?" Lucy asked, throwing her arm over her eyes in dramatic fashion. "I'll never be able to look Lady Featherstone in the eye again."

Charity knew all too well the feeling of humiliation and shame that was likely burning through Lucy at the knowledge she may become the subject of unwanted gossip. It had become her daily companion until she had finally decided she no longer cared and would turn her attention to doing whatever it was she wished.

"Fear not, my dear," she reassured her friend. "I've been

scandalizing polite society for years, and I can still hold the dowager's gaze with the stone-cold precision of a statue."

Indeed, she took delight in staring down that august, meddlesome lady whenever she could. She considered herself a reminder of the havoc that could be wreaked by wagging tongues.

"I suppose I'm making amends for my scandalous ways by marrying the earl," Lucy said faintly, her countenance pale in contrast to her mahogany hair, her vivid eyes rendered a more vibrant shade of green.

Charity couldn't help but wonder if Lucy truly wanted to marry the earl or if she felt as if she had been trapped into doing so. The manor house had been ablaze with talk of Lucy and Rexingham's betrothal when she'd returned from her sojourn with Wilton. Rexingham and his sister Bette, meanwhile, had already departed. It was all rather odd to Charity's mind. Troubling, too.

"I must say that when I had the notion for this house party first in mind, I couldn't have predicted that it would lead to betrothals," Vivi interjected thoughtfully from her chair by the fireplace, her words echoing Charity's own suspicions. Golden-haired and faultlessly elegant, the only duchess among them was not just the reason they had all become friends; she was also compassionate and generous. "My original intention was to gather like minds and increase the membership and reach of the Lady's Suffrage Society."

"And you've done that as well," Clementine reassured their friend and hostess from her perch on a nearby window seat, looking impeccable this morning with her dark hair swept back from her face into an intricate coiffure, her silk gown bedecked with flowers.

Vivi's smile turned wistful. "I'm very pleased that you've all decided to join us. However, I am quite surprised. I didn't think you were particularly marriage-minded, Lucy."

44

"Lord Rexingham has persuaded me to see the error of my ways," Lucy offered, her tone painfully polite.

"Persuasion? Is that what you're calling it?" Madeline teased her.

Lucy sent a glare in her sister's direction. "Yes, dearest. It is."

"Did the earl catch a bee in your skirts?" Charity asked, aiming to keep their conversation lighthearted.

By now, the incident between Clementine and the Marquess of Dorset and a bee, which had necessitated their betrothal, was infamous. It had also been the start of a true love match for Clementine and Dorset. She was quite content with her marquess, and well she should be, for Dorset doted on Clementine equally. The way he looked at her was a source of envy for Charity. Not because she begrudged her friend happiness and love. But because she'd once believed herself capable of achieving it.

No longer.

"Thankfully not," Lucy said.

For some reason, Viscount Wilton rose in Charity's mind. Strong, deadly handsome, and stern. A forbidding Adonis who was all harsh angles and edges and proper perfection and yet possessed such a vulnerable side. A side he'd allowed her to glimpse earlier in the boathouse and, later, at the lake. Until the moment he had closed that part of him away, rather as if he were slamming a door. And then he had all but fled from her as if she were a sorceress intent upon casting an evil spell upon him for all eternity. She firmly banished all thoughts of him.

"Sometimes, the appropriate stimulus is all that is required to change one's mind," Edith was saying. "The breeding habits of sheep, for instance, suggest—"

"Oh, Edith," Charity interrupted, not wanting to endure another lengthy soliloquy from her dear friend concerning livestock. "Pray don't tell us about sheep mating again. I'll never be able to look at a lamb in the same way again as it is."

"It couldn't have been as bad as when she tried to expound on the vagaries of whale dung," Madeline added with a delicate shudder.

"But I've already told you that ambergris isn't specifically whale dung," Edith argued, frowning from where she was seated on a divan, a treatise of some sort open in her lap. "It's a substance found within the feces of the Physeter Macrocephalus."

"You can try to explain it to us in every language you know, my dear, but I'm afraid it won't help your case," Charity said gently. "Let's play a favorite game of mine called Pretend It Never Happened and carry on with our conversation."

"What were we talking about?" Clementine asked with a frown.

"Lucy's marriage, of course," Madeline offered cheerfully, her grin suggesting she was enjoying her sister's misery.

Lucy drummed her fingers on the armrests of her chair. "I'd prefer it if we wouldn't, truly. It's months away, and I don't want to think about it any longer than necessary. Mother has already given me a headache by making an endless number of plans concerning my trousseau and dress. I had to listen to her drone on about Brussels lace and myrtle flowers for an entire hour."

Charity winced. "That truly sounds wretched. Given the choice between listening to a discussion on lace and flowers or sheep mating, I'm afraid I'd have to endure the sheep mating."

"The crossbreeding of sheep is quite interesting," Edith insisted. "I've read a great deal about it."

Darling, scholarly, odd Edith.

"Of course you have, dear," Charity said, patting her

friend's arm in consoling fashion. "And you know I adore you, but I'll never quite understand your affection for certain subjects."

Her mind drifted again, thinking of Lucy's impending nuptials to the earl. Her friend's untenable position was one Charity would thankfully never find herself in. She didn't want to marry. Not ever. She was perfectly contented in her life as it was. But then an insidious, wicked little thought came suddenly to mind, accompanied by the memory of Lord Wilton's intoxicating masculine scent and his beautifully sculpted lips. Perhaps what she needed was a lover…

No, that was wrong. She didn't dare risk it. And even if she did, Lord Wilton was hardly the sort to be interested in a clandestine tryst. He was far too proper. His sensibilities would never allow such a lapse in propriety. As much as his unusual eyes had devoured her, he'd never made the slightest hint of an inappropriate move to be familiar. Not one misplaced touch or kiss.

But still, she couldn't help but wonder what it would feel like, his mouth on hers. His hands not just on her waist, but everywhere. Gliding up her ribs to cup the swells of her breasts. Lifting up her skirts. On her leg. Higher.

Charity's face went hot, and an ache pulsed to life between her thighs, one that made her shift on her seat in an effort to assuage it as her friends chattered on about the morning's betrothal announcement and the surrounding scandal. When their discussion completed its circle and returned to the dowager marchioness fainting into a heap on the floor, Charity happily surrendered herself to the satisfying thought of her nemesis crumpling in an embarrassing display.

"I would have dearly liked to see Lady Featherstone swooning this morning," she said. "It must have been quite a sight. Pray don't take offense, Edith dear. It's just that your mother spread that dreadful rumor about me posing as naked as a babe for that Venus painting, and I've never forgiven her for it."

"I know, Charity, and I'm so sorry." Edith shook her head, looking mournful. "I've asked her never to repeat it."

"And I love you for your loyalty, dear friend." Charity forced a smile she didn't feel for her friend's benefit—it wasn't sweet Edith's fault that her mother was a gossiping dragon. "Fortunately, I don't have to worry about gossip and being proper. I have no intention of ever marrying."

"Never, my dear?" Vivi asked, her brow furrowed. "Are you certain?"

She shuddered. "I've never been more certain of anything in my life."

Ainsley had more than cured her of any romantic delusions she may have once possessed. But another errant thought wormed its way into her mind again as their conversation carried on. The one that told her there was no reason she couldn't take a lover. Why she couldn't seize all the freedoms a man easily and greedily took.

And perhaps she would.

All she needed to do was find a suitable candidate. A rake. A rogue.

Anyone other than Viscount Wilton.

~

GRINDING HIS MOLARS, Neville strode into the Sherborne Manor music room, only to find it empty. For the second time in as many days, he had lost his niece. The day was dreary and raining, which meant it unlikely she was wandering outdoors. And so he was conducting an impromptu tour of the massive manor house in search of her.

Margaret was still quite irritated with him for refusing to even consider the possibility of her visiting the Continent with or without the maddening Lady Charity. They had argued the night before on their way down to dinner. They had quarreled again this morning at breakfast. She had spent the afternoon in the drawing room with most of the other ladies in attendance, deep in a discussion concerning a leaflet being drafted for dissemination by the Lady's Suffrage Society. But where she had gone when that gathering had dispersed remained a mystery he was intent upon solving.

He disliked when they were at odds, and the devil of it was, Lady Charity's words had been churning in his mind ever since the day before when they had talked. *Not every woman wishes to marry and find herself turned into a broodmare,* she'd said. It was hardly what he wanted for Margaret. What he wanted for her was happiness and security. He wanted to fulfill his obligation to Wentworth.

But after breakfast, he had settled down to read quietly in his chamber, and he had reached a shocking realization. He hadn't asked Margaret what *she* had wanted. As he sat in the comfortable stillness of his guest bedchamber, he'd realized further that Lady Charity wasn't entirely wrong in her assessment of him.

He *had* assumed he knew what Margaret wanted. He had, and rather high-handedly, taken his brother's wishes and his own good intentions and used them to supplant his niece's hopes for her future. He hadn't asked.

He should have done so.

He *would* do so. But first, he had to find her.

Neville ventured through a tranquil sitting room, also empty, and then dipped into the library. Within the cavernous room, books lined the walls, and a bank of windows overlooked the vast expanse of the Sherborne

Manor park. The view would have been breathtaking were it not for something else that stole his attention.

Or rather, someone.

A golden goddess who was dressed in a purple gown that looked as if it had been fashioned to bring all mortal men to their knees before her. The bodice clung to her nipped waist and drew attention to the generous swells of her breasts. Breasts that he knew from the day before were even fuller and riper without the constraints of her corset.

She was reclining on a Grecian couch that must have hailed from the earlier part of the century from the looks of it, cradling her cheek in one palm as she rested on her side, an open book on the tufted velvet cushion before her.

Cobalt eyes flicked up and over him, and he felt that gaze as if it were a caress. His chest seized. Desire slammed into him, so potent that he swayed on his feet. He wondered if she could see it written on his face and prayed she couldn't.

"Lord Wilton," she said without bothering to right herself into a more ladylike position.

Not that he had expected her to move. He had been watching her for the duration of the house party, attracted to her undeniable beauty from the start, even if he was equally repelled by her boisterous nature. But he couldn't shake the feeling that it had only been yesterday that he had truly seen her for the first time. He knew the rebellious spirit within her, and he suspected he knew the reason for it, too.

He bowed. "Lady Charity."

When he straightened, he stared at her, thinking that he understood all too well why the artist had chosen her for his muse. If he had been blessed with such a skill, he would have been tempted to paint her like this.

Venus at Rest, he thought as a sharp stab of envy speared him for the man who had spent enough time in her presence to bring her to life on canvas. The man who had seen her body without a single stitch of clothing to obscure his view of her feminine beauty.

That last thought made him set his teeth on edge.

"Have you come looking for a book?" she asked calmly, as if he weren't presently drowning in unmitigated longing and jealousy united.

He blinked, recalling belatedly the reason he had come to the library in the first place, which hadn't had a thing to do with admiring her. "Have you seen my niece this afternoon?"

"Lost her again, have you?" Lady Charity's full rose-pink lips tipped upward in a smug smile.

"Do you find it amusing?" he asked stiffly, suddenly aware he was still standing in the presence of a lady.

His ingrained sense of gentlemanly behavior forced him to move nearer to her against his better judgment. He found an overstuffed armchair and sank into it since Lady Charity didn't seem inclined to rise from her position, regardless of how unmannerly it was.

"That you've lost your niece, or that you're wandering about like a lost puppy?"

He gripped the arms of the chair in irritation. "I'm hardly a puppy, madam."

She turned a page with her index finger, her smile deepening. "A kitten, then."

He didn't feel kittenish at all in her presence. He felt rather like a lion. One who wanted to gather her up and carry her away with him. One who wanted to devour her, utterly. But that was foolishness, and he was nothing if not civilized. Fortunately, he could tamp down all such inconvenient urges with ruthless determination.

"Have you seen her?" he ground out.

"No need to be vexed with me, my lord. I'm not the one who has lost Margaret."

She was the most vexing woman of his acquaintance.

Admittedly, that circle was currently small, and quite intentionally too.

"Can you not at least sit up when you converse with me, madam?" he asked tightly.

It was as if the connection—that rare and precious dismantling of the walls they both kept around themselves—of the day before had been severed. And that was for the best, because he couldn't afford to like this woman. She was far too dangerous.

Dangerous to his sanity.

To his celibacy.

To his niece.

To his reputation.

The list could go on, but Neville hardly had patience or time to continue in his mind. He had an errant niece to locate.

"Why should I?" Lady Charity asked calmly. "I'm quite comfortable as I am. Besides, you are the one who has intruded upon my solitude for the second day in a row. I'm beginning to think this is a new habit of yours, along with puns."

"And I'm beginning to think it the greatest irony of all time that a woman so lacking in proper behavior ought to have the surname Manners," he snapped.

The flash of hurt on her countenance—so swiftly gone, it may not have been there at all—sank into him like a barb. He wasn't irritated with her as much as he was himself. For his inconvenient attraction to such an unsuitable woman, for making a muck of things with Margaret, for realizing he may have been wrong when he had been trying so very hard to be right.

Lady Charity closed her book with a loud thump, her gaze thunderous as it met his. "I haven't seen your niece since the Lady's Suffrage meeting earlier. But it's hardly surprising she's hiding from you, given your lack of joy."

Lack of joy?

He was joyful.

Sometimes.

Very well, perhaps only occasionally. His life had been spent in a great deal of loneliness and loss, and both had made their mark upon him. And add to that the burden of always having been strange. The odd brother. The disappointment. The vessel for his father's anger. The lad who tripped over his tongue and hid from the world, only to become the man who locked himself away until life had intervened in the form of his garrulous niece.

"You might have told me so," Neville said curtly, preparing to rise. "If you'll excuse me, my lady. I must continue in my search."

"Wait."

He stilled, his hands gripping the armrests with so much force it was a miracle he hadn't snapped them off. "Yes, Lady Charity?"

With a lithe grace, she swung her feet and skirts to the floor, elbowing herself into a sitting position. No easy feat, he suspected, given her corset and cumbersome underpinnings. And yet she made it look effortless. Likely because she had done it many times before. And perversely, the thought of her lounging around reading a book wearing nothing at all filled his head.

"I'll accompany you," she told him.

His trousers suddenly seemed far too snug, along with his neckcloth. It was fortuitous indeed that she couldn't read his lecherous thoughts from his countenance. That he didn't blurt the wicked inner workings of his mind along with puns.

"That won't be necessary, my lady."

The less time he spent in this maddening woman's company, the better. He needed distance.

"I know it's not necessary." She stood, shaking out her skirts. "But I'll offer my aid just the same. You seem hopelessly inept at keeping her under your watchful eye."

A few stray golden curls had slipped free from her coiffure. His fingers itched to tuck them behind her ear, and he had no notion of why. Neville shot to his feet as well, rather as if his chair had suddenly turned to lava.

"I can assure you I'm not inept," he countered, stung by her assessment. "At least, not under ordinary circumstances. I'll admit that this is the first country house party I've attended in many years and the only one I've attended since I've become Margaret's guardian."

And he was beginning to realize he knew absolutely nothing about twenty-year-old young ladies. Which made perfect sense, because the last time he had spoken with a twenty-year-old lady, he'd been a shy, awkward twenty-year-old himself.

"As I've been to any number of them, it would behoove you to accept my offer, Lord Wilton," Lady Charity said calmly, gliding toward him.

He wanted to tell her to call him Neville. Just for the sheer joy of hearing his given name uttered in her husky voice. But he stifled the urge. For she was the sort of female who would take an entire carriage if he offered her a horseshoe.

"Truly, you needn't. I'll find her."

"Don't sound so dismayed," she chided, sweeping past him. "What is the worst harm that can be done in your accepting my aid, hmm?"

There was a great deal of harm. For instance, the longer he was alone with her, the more tempted he became to claim those sultry lips with his. To kiss her until she was breathless. To do far more than that.

"I'm not certain it's wise for us to conduct a search together," he managed past the warring misgiving and lust roaring within him.

She whirled about to face him, a study in irritation, her eyes snapping with fire. "Why not?"

Her scent chose that moment to curl around him. Not cloying, but inviting. And sweet God, he couldn't think of a single thing to say. He couldn't even think of a single word.

"Well?" she demanded. "It doesn't look as if you've been succeeding on your own."

He took a step forward against his will. It was the fault of his feet, really. They were taking him somewhere his mind didn't want him to be. A place where the rest of his body very much wanted him to be.

Closer to her.

CHAPTER 5

*C*harity tried to quell the rising surge of awareness
threatening to overwhelm her as Viscount Wilton
strode toward her. Everything within her urged her to flee in
the opposite direction, and yet she couldn't. She didn't. She
wouldn't.

Because he was looking at her as if he wanted to consume
her, his pale eyes burning with intensity, and she wanted
nothing more than to cast herself into his arms and discover
what his mouth would feel like on hers. Taking hers. Would
it be gentle and hesitant like his puns, or would it be deep
and possessive? Or would it be something in between?

"Why shouldn't I accompany you?" she asked when he
stopped before her, so tall and strong and deliciously male.

The breathless quality of her voice nettled her. She didn't
want him to know how badly his proximity affected her. She
wanted him to think her impervious.

He said nothing for a moment, his countenance harsh and
grim, his full lips pinched into a severe line, as if he were
concentrating on something of the utmost importance.

And then, finally, he spoke.

"Because it would be unwise."

His deep voice had taken on a raspy quality that sent a frisson of awareness down Charity's spine. Warmth blossomed. Despite the coolness of the dreary day, she was on fire. Burning up, and all because of him.

"Why?" she pressed, daring him to answer her.

To tell her the truth she could see blazing in his eyes.

He crowded her, his woodsy and citrus scent filling her lungs. She inhaled sharply, wanting that scent. Wanting more of him. His body seemed to radiate heat, and he stepped near, bending his head so that his lips were at her ear. Not touching her. Not even grazing her when he spoke, but they may as well have for the impact he had on her.

"Because," he said softly with a voice like rich, melted butter, "I can't be in your presence without thinking about what you looked like at the lake yesterday morning, almost naked."

She released the breath she hadn't realized she'd been holding, her nipples tightening to hard points of awareness beneath her corset, a heady ache blossoming between her thighs. It was the last reason she had expected him to give. And the only reason that made desire rain over her, causing her to sway into him until her hands flitted to his shoulders for purchase.

They stayed that way for a moment, his muscles searing her through his coat, his breath falling hot on her ear.

She was going to do something that was foolish, and she knew it. But she was going to do it anyway.

She turned her head so that their noses nearly grazed each other, and still, he didn't withdraw. He remained impossibly close, his breath coasting over her mouth now.

Holding his unusual gaze, she said, "Then perhaps you should see me when I'm fully naked, Lord Wilton."

The brazen invitation slid from her lips, and she didn't

know why, only that he'd pushed her beyond the pale. She thought he might move away from her. That she might have horrified or disgusted him with her forwardness. But he remained where he was, and instead of pushing her from him, he settled his hands on her waist in a possessive hold she couldn't help but enjoy.

"What a shocking thing to say, Lady Charity," he said, his voice low, his gaze dropping to her mouth.

"Have I horrified you?" she asked breathlessly.

What she really meant to say was *kiss me. Kiss me now, despite all sense of reason, all sense of right and wrong. Kiss me even if we could be caught at any moment. Regardless of rules and scandal.*

But she didn't say any of that, because this was Viscount Wilton, and she wasn't even sure he had the capacity for such boldness. And also because a part of her *liked* him. Liked him far more than she should. And she didn't want to push him beyond the limits of his own comfort any more than she already had.

"You have an appalling lack of concern for propriety," he murmured, but there was no bite, no sting in his words. There was only the sweet, velvet promise of something more. Something forbidden.

His head lowered, and he skimmed his lips over hers in the barest whisper of a kiss. Scarcely any pressure. And dear heavens, that simple brush of his mouth over hers was nearly enough to bring her to her knees. She whimpered, the sound torn from her, scarcely recognizing herself. She'd never felt so much yearning, building up, filling her.

He withdrew, staring at her, his gaze hard and unyielding. "And yet I find myself hopelessly drawn to you anyway."

His tone was unyielding; his words were stern. He was a man at odds with himself, wanting what he shouldn't want and daring what he shouldn't dare. They stared at each other, and her lips parted in welcome, his to take.

His head dipped again, and once more, his mouth moved against hers with soft, tantalizing insistence. Once again, the touch was light and barely there. Teasing, taunting, tempting. But it wasn't enough. One of her hands slid from his shoulder until she grasped a handful of his necktie. Her fingers wrapped around it, and she tugged, pulling him closer, forcing his mouth to take hers more fully.

It was an invitation he accepted with a low growl, his lips pressing into hers, his hand moving from her waist to cup her nape, holding her there as he ravished her mouth with a kiss so hungry and powerful that her knees threatened to give. The proper, polite veneer fell away. It was as if she had unleashed a sensual beast he'd been hiding carefully within, and he was intent upon seizing what she had so readily offered.

She opened for him fully with a soft moan, needing more, needing his tongue.

He sensed what she desired, licking into her mouth so that she could taste him, a sweet and heady blend of man and tea. Their kiss deepened, turning into something else. Something unprecedented. Another breathy moan left her, and she returned his kiss with all the desire shimmering within her. It was as if, at any moment, she might catch flame. He astounded her. He pleased her. He kissed her slowly and deeply, with maddening precision, as if he savored her.

Charity had been kissed before, but never like *this*.

She was lost in sensation. Helpless to think of anything other than Wilton as the rest of the house party—heavens, the rest of the world—fell away. He kissed her and kissed her until her lips were deliciously bruised and she could scarcely catch her breath. And then he dragged his mouth along her jaw, kissing a trail of pure fire to her ear.

"We shouldn't be doing this," he murmured.

"No," she agreed. "We shouldn't."

He nuzzled her jaw, his lips finding her throat.

She tilted her head back, giving him as much of her skin as she could. He kissed a fiery trail across her neck, open-mouthed and hot. Her knees trembled. She clutched him more tightly to keep from crumpling to the Axminster in a puddle of silk. Wilton's mouth was casting a spell over her.

But not just his mouth. It was every part of him. It was his springtime forest scent, his lean, muscled strength so at odds with the dour figure he often presented, his hands coasting over her body as if he couldn't touch her enough. It was his height, his nearness, the intoxicating heat his body radiated into hers. It was the gentle rasp of his golden hair against her cheek as he raked his teeth over her collarbone.

The hand he'd left at her waist traveled. Slid up her bodice, over boning and silk, and cupped her breast as if it belonged there, his thumb unerringly finding her pebbled nipple and rubbing slow, maddening circles over it. The pressure made her arch into him, seeking more. Wanting his bare hand on her skin, the smooth caress of his thumb directly on her nipple instead of separated from it. Just *wanting*. Oh, how he made her long for what she could not have.

He made her long to shed the barriers of her endless layers of garments. He made her want to lie with him in a bed and do things she'd only read about. He made her want so badly, so fiercely, that it was an ache throbbing deep within her, one she knew could only be assuaged in one impossible way.

She couldn't give herself to Viscount Wilton. Couldn't ask him to share her bed. Charity prided herself on her lack of adherence to propriety and rules, but even she knew when she'd gone too far. Already, several scandals had unfolded at her friend Vivi's house party. Charity couldn't make one more, regardless of the temptation.

Sanity seemed to return to them both at the same moment.

They jolted apart, both of them breathless, their gazes clashing. Wilton's lips were dark from their kisses, and his eyes were glazed with passion. She thought she must be a mirror of him, a portrait of a woman who had just had her first true taste of desire—and from the least likely source.

Ainsley had never made her feel this restless yearning. He'd never kissed her or touched her with such passion, as if he existed only to please her, to run his hands and lips over her body and claim her as his.

She was shaken.

Badly.

"I must apologize," Wilton said formally, as if he had inadvertently stepped on her train in a ballroom instead of feeding her his tongue and kissing her until she had almost melted and forgotten her own name.

She licked her lips, tasting him, trying to find the proper words. To act as if she was impervious to his advances, completely unaffected. Failing utterly.

He swallowed, his Adam's apple bobbing above the neck-cloth that had been left comically askew by her own fevered tugging. "You needn't say anything, Lady Charity. I'm appalled by my own actions. I can assure you that nothing like this will happen again."

Oh, but she wanted it to. Longed for it desperately. How could he stand there looking so unruffled, issuing polite apologies, when she couldn't even think?

Charity inhaled a shaky breath, wondering what to say.

She was spared the decision when the library door clicked open. She and Wilton turned as one toward the sound. Thankfully, the intruder crossing over the threshold was none other than the viscount's missing niece, Margaret, who was either too naïve or too unobservant to realize she had just intruded on a heated moment between her uncle and Charity.

"Uncle," Margaret greeted with a sunny smile. "I've been looking for you." Belatedly, she took note of Charity standing not far from him. "Oh, Lady Charity. How are you today?"

Quite thoroughly ruined by your uncle's kisses, she thought uncharitably.

But she pinned a welcoming smile of her own to her lips instead. "I'm well, thank you, Miss Astley. How are you faring?"

"Splendidly now," she chirped, still blithely unaware of the undercurrent in the room. "We're going to be playing parlor games this afternoon on account of the rain. Will you both be joining us?"

"Parlor games?" Wilton repeated, his voice and countenance both making no secret of his distaste for such frivolity.

And something about his detached, icy reserve in the wake of the fiery kisses they had just shared irked her. Pushed her beyond restraint and good sense.

"Your uncle was just telling me how much he enjoys parlor games," Charity said breezily, meeting the viscount's shocked gaze without flinching. "I'm sure he would love to join you, my dear."

"He was?" Margaret stopped short of them in the cavernous library, looking ethereally lovely, despite the frown marring her brow.

The resemblance between uncle and niece was uncanny. Miss Astley might have been Wilton's daughter, were it not for their age difference. She had the same hair and unusual eyes, the same proud nose and tall and willowy form, though she was still quite a bit shorter than her uncle. It was plain, however, that Wilton was too young to have sired a twenty-year-old daughter. For the first time, it occurred to Charity that most unattached bachelors, when suddenly burdened with a spirited young lady as a ward, might have run in the opposite direction or, at the very least, pawned her off onto an accommodating, distant female relation.

Wilton clearly loved his niece. He also was clearly flummoxed by her.

"Oh yes, he was," Charity confirmed cheerfully. "I do so hope the both of you enjoy yourselves."

But when she would have made good on her hasty escape, fleeing from the maddening presence of one too-handsome viscount whose kisses had left her knees weak, his voice stopped her.

"Indeed, I was. However, Lady Charity was sharing a similar confidence."

Her gaze swung to him. "I was?"

He grinned, showing the presence of two devastating dimples that somehow had been, heretofore, hiding on his austere mien. "Why, Lady Charity, can you not recall?"

She couldn't help but to wonder crossly where the nervous, awkward lord who blurted puns had gone. In his place was a leonine seducer, a sharp-tongued, handsome devil who delivered a checkmate without a blink.

"Perhaps you're mistaken, my lord," she gritted through clamped teeth, her smile feeling more like a snarl.

Parlor games had never interested her, and she could only assume that some of the younger ladies in attendance were playing them. At five-and-twenty, Charity truly couldn't be bothered with such nonsense.

"No." He shook his head slowly, his dimples deepening as if he was enjoying her discomfiture. "I don't think I am. I recall distinctly your saying that you could scarcely restrain yourself in your excitement."

She ground her molars at his thinly veiled dig at her reaction to his wicked kisses. At the cheek of the man, speaking with such obvious innuendo before his niece, who was watching their interaction with a look of perplexed concern.

"I think your lordship has a faulty memory," she suggested tightly.

"Uncle's memory is remarkably faultless," Margaret interjected. "He remembers the most minute details from when he was just a lad."

Of course he did.

She didn't doubt it.

Charity glowered at his infuriatingly smug, handsome face. "Perhaps it is his hearing that is the problem, then. It happens when one reaches an advanced age."

His eyes narrowed.

"Advanced age?" Margaret chuckled. "Why, Uncle is only one-and-thirty. Hardly advanced."

Charity already knew his age because of the heartbreaking story he had shared the day before concerning his younger brother who had drowned. But she couldn't well reveal that to his niece, so she feigned surprise instead.

"Ah, perhaps not as ancient as I supposed him to be, then," she said, sparing him another glance.

If his glare had been a dagger, it would have been buried between her ribs. Excellent. Let him stew. Being at odds with him felt far more comfortable than being ravished in his arms had. Because she wanted the latter far too much.

"Not ancient at all, madam," he said, his voice clipped. "Since our hostess has seen fit to entertain us with parlor games, I reckon I should escort both you and my niece to the drawing room."

Charity suppressed a sigh. She didn't want to linger in Wilton's tempting presence a moment longer than necessary, but she also didn't want him to know how very unsettled his kisses and his embrace had left her.

"Very well," she allowed grudgingly. "I suppose you may as well lead the way, Lord Wilton. Because surely you are joining us, are you not?"

A muscle in his jaw clenched. He didn't want to go to the drawing rooms for parlor games any more than Charity did. However, like her, he was unwilling to show his vulnerability.

"Why is a gooseberry tart like a bad sixpence?" he asked in a sure sign of how unsettled he was at the notion of engaging in so much social tomfoolery.

Charity knew a moment of shame at having forced his hand.

"Because it's not currant?" Margaret asked.

"You've heard that one before, dear girl," he said, proffering an arm in his niece's direction and another in Charity's. "Come then, let us heed the hangman's call."

"Oh, Uncle." Margaret laughed. "The hangman, truly. It's just a bit of fun."

Charity reluctantly settled her hand in the crook of the viscount's arm, absorbing the tension in his form. "Lead the way, my lord."

She had a suspicion that the parlor games were going to go dreadfully.

She hoped she was wrong.

～

It was excruciating.

First, they had played forfeits. By the time charades had begun—a frivolous game for the young, and one in which he damned well didn't care to indulge—Neville slipped from the drawing room, secure in the knowledge that Margaret was at least surrounded by a chamber filled with fellow houseguests and not out gallivanting across the countryside or plotting to elope with a groom.

As the raucous and delighted voices calling out guesses faded away down the hall while he strode in the opposite direction, a new sound reached him. The undeniable flurry of silk skirts and the soft footfalls of a woman.

"Going somewhere, Lord Wilton?"

The voice behind him was every bit as familiar. It was a voice he swore would haunt his most erotic dreams from now until eternity. Particularly after those fever-inducing kisses they had shared in the library. He still didn't know what demon had come over him. Didn't know what the hell he had been thinking.

Neville paused and spun to face Lady Charity Manners, who was hastening after him with a determined expression on her face. He might have known that he wouldn't have escaped with such ease.

He wanted to heft her over his shoulder and carry her away to his bedchamber. To kiss her until neither of them could speak. To strip her out of that damned enticing gown and lick every inch of her body until she was writhing with need and she was begging him to take her.

He shook his head, chasing the foolish fancies. "Lady Charity. I thought you were engrossed in the parlor games."

It was a polite way of asking her why the devil she was following him. Dogging him. Making him long for her with a desperation that had him tempted to throw every last modicum of propriety he believed in away.

"I'd far prefer to take the air," she said, stopping before him, a lush temptation he itched to touch. "I'm going for a walk."

Where was the aunt who was chaperoning her? Did she realize what a hellion she had on her hands? Part of him was convinced that Lady Charity Manners on a walk would devolve into her running naked through the woods. Someone needed to take the woman in hand.

Not him.

Obviously.

He couldn't be trusted to be alone with her in a library without attempting to ravish her. Heat crept up his throat at the reminder of his inability to control himself. At her response to him. Good God, if he didn't take care, he was going to be sporting a cockstand right here in the midst of the hall, whilst half the guests in attendance played bloody charades.

He tried to think of something suitably confident to say and couldn't summon a single word.

"Why is the letter P like a Roman emperor?" he found himself asking, his voice strained.

Her brow furrowed, as if she were trying to decipher the answer to his pun. As if she were truly humoring him.

And he wanted to kiss her again. Kiss her and kiss her and never stop.

This was beginning to become concerning. Hell, he had advanced well beyond concern, proceeding to the cliffs of doom.

"Hmm," she murmured, looking puzzled. "I can't think of a reason."

"Because it's Near-*o*." And gads, it wasn't one of his finer puns, the play on Nero and the letters' positions in the alphabet. He couldn't seem to help himself in any capacity whenever he was in proximity to Lady Charity Manners.

But then, something astonishing happened.

She laughed. And God, the sound of that laughter. It was musical and bright, airy and tinkling, and it fell over his skin like a caress, every bit as wicked and potent in its effect on him. He had to suck in a breath and remind himself that they stood in the midst of the hall, domestics bustling quietly about in the background. That this was decidedly not a place where he could press his mouth to her smiling lips and seize a small piece of her wild abandon for himself.

"You liked that one?" he asked, bemused.

There was no denying it—the sparkle of levity somehow rendered her eyes a deeper shade of blue. She'd been amused. And she wasn't laughing at him, but *with* him.

"It was one of your most clever puns yet," she said, smiling at him, then catching the fullness of her lower lip in her teeth, as if seeking to quell her reaction.

Too late for that. He'd seen it. She couldn't take it back. And Neville suddenly felt as if he were ten feet tall.

"Thank you," he said softly, and they stared at each other in a new silence.

Not an uncomfortable one, but rather, a silence that spoke volumes.

"I think I'd like to take the air as well," he told her.

And in the same moment, she said in a rush, "Perhaps you would like to accompany me, my lord."

He found himself smiling back at her, hopelessly charmed, and offered her his arm for the second time that day. "Yes, I would like to do so. Just as long as you promise me not to turn into a mermaid, that is."

A becoming flush stole over her high cheekbones as she settled her hand on his arm as if it belonged there. "I make no promises, Lord Wilton."

And God help him, he wanted it to belong there. Wanted her hand on him. For a wild moment, he envisioned those dainty, pale fingers encircling his prick. And then he struck down the unworthy thought. Lady Charity was a lady. A bold and daring one, yes, but a lady just the same. He had to treat her thusly.

"Do you need a wrap?" he asked solicitously as he guided them to the door.

The rain of earlier had subsided, but the skies remained leaden and dull, dreary with the portent of more on the horizon. The air, though it was summer here in Yorkshire, could possess something of a nip on damp days in particular. The day before had been unseasonably warm, which he supposed was probably part of the reason for her morning jaunt in the lake. Surely she hadn't gone this morning.

"Thank you, but no," she reassured him. "The drawing room was such a crush, and with all that movement for charades, I find I'm quite overheated. If the air is cool, it will be a relief."

He felt the same way, but it didn't have a blessed thing to do with the drawing room or the parlor games being played within. He hadn't participated in any of them anyhow. No, indeed. He was overheated because of the woman on his arm.

Because her beauty was unfair. And because he had never known temptation quite like the sort that she presented.

"Of course," he said with what he hoped was a glib air, not that he had ever managed to affect one in his entire misbegotten life.

Why should he be able to do so now?

But he guided her out of the main house after they both retrieved their hats just the same. From there, they ventured into the side garden where the boxwood maze had been elaborately carved out, a meandering gravel path the only guide. They walked in an almost companionable silence, interrupted by nothing more strenuous than the crunch of their mutual footfalls.

A bird winged overhead, its cry echoing around them, joining the trill of other birds singing in the absence of the rain.

"It would seem we aren't the only ones seeking a respite

after the morning's storms," he said, taking in the beauty of their surroundings.

For whilst it paled in comparison to that of Lady Charity, it was a far safer place to direct his attention. He couldn't be tempted to kiss the rosebushes or to carry the hedges back to his bedchamber.

"I confess, I thought you would be terribly cross with me for the manner in which I cozened you into attending forfeits and charades," Lady Charity said calmly at his side.

He slanted a glance in her direction. "I'll own, I wasn't pleased. Was I mistaken in supposing you were attempting to get even with me for my lack of restraint in the library?"

"Lack of restraint." Her lips twitched. "Is that what you're calling it, my lord?"

What was it about this woman that made him feel as if she were privy to the world's greatest sally, leaving him on tenterhooks wondering when she might deign to let him know what it was? She was maddening, intoxicating, alluring.

Insufferable.

He wanted her, and he hated himself for wanting her. He desired her, and it was all her fault.

"What else would you have me call it?" he ventured.

"I do believe you kissed me, Lord Wilton. And more than once. Quite pleasantly too, I might add."

The way she said those words made a bolt of lust slide straight through him. She'd liked his kisses? He was gratified, because those kisses had ruined him. He'd spent the first interminable hour of forfeits thinking of nothing else.

"Might you call me Neville?" he suggested, and he didn't know why, other than for the sheer pleasure of hearing his given name in her husky voice. Of having it on her lips, as surely as his kisses had been.

"Neville, then," she agreed. "And you must also call me Charity."

"Only when we're alone, of course," he rushed to add. "Which won't be often."

Or, if he was wise, ever again.

But his presence at her side just now was surely proof of his shocking dearth of wisdom.

"Of course," she agreed easily. "You looked terribly unamused by the merriments earlier."

"Hmm." He offered a noncommittal hum, all he was willing to utter in that regard.

Did that mean she'd been watching him as surreptitiously as he had her? Neville thought it wisest not to ask, so he turned his attention instead toward the greenery surrounding them, along with the clouds passing in the distance.

"You dislike parlor games?" she guessed, because of course she couldn't allow the silence to stretch on uninterrupted.

"I dislike most of society's trappings," he answered truthfully. "I never thought to have to involve myself with such matters. I was always pleased to keep my attention on my investments and my own estate. My brother was the heir, and when he inherited the title, I never thought to see the day that I would be the one squiring Margaret about."

His voice broke on the last few words, an embarrassing show of emotion that he didn't like but couldn't seem to help.

Charity's fingers tightened on his arm. "I'm sorry, my lord. You've known a great deal of loss in your life."

"Likely not more than anyone else," he said, attempting a smile for her benefit.

Wentworth had been thirteen years his senior, but despite their differences in age and temperament, Neville and his brother had been close. Wentworth's loss still left a gaping chasm inside him, and he knew from experience that the hole would never entirely be filled.

"Two brothers," she said quietly at his side.

"And a sister," he added. "Violet was only two when she caught a vicious lung infection and died."

"I'm sorry. Little wonder you're so removed. You'd have to be, to have lost nearly your entire family and yet endure."

Her assumption was natural, and if he had any sense at all, he would allow her to think it the truth. It hardly mattered anyway.

"I've always been this way," he blurted, and he could have kicked himself for the confession.

He might have allowed her to believe him normal. But there was nothing ordinary about the way in which his mind functioned. There never had been. His own father and mother had reassured him of that. He'd endured far too many disappointed sermons from his mother and too many angry tirades from his father about being an unnatural child to believe he'd ever been the way everyone else was.

He was simply himself, and even if no one else could accept it for longer than a few months, he had been able to accept himself. That, too, had taken time and a great deal of studious reflection. For many years, his self-loathing had threatened to consume him.

"What do you mean, *this way?*" she asked, stopping them on the path and facing him, her countenance pensive, almost troubled.

A sudden attack of nervousness washed over him. He couldn't bear to explain.

"Think nothing of it," he forced out with manufactured calm. "Let us continue our walk, shall we?"

"No." Her look turned mulish, as well he should have known it would. "Explain, if you please."

"I should think it obvious." His terrible puns. The way he

froze. The rapid beating of his heart, his inability to converse smoothly.

It was why he did everything he could to keep away from all forms of society.

Wentworth had been smooth and charming, and everyone had been drawn to him. He'd been the perfect son, the perfect viscount. Their father had never allowed Neville to forget it.

But Charity wasn't graciously allowing him to escape or change the subject. Instead, she was holding his gaze, placing a hand on his coat sleeve from where he had unceremoniously shrugged her off.

"Your puns, do you mean?" she asked softly.

He closed his eyes for a moment, shutting out the sight of her, so beautiful and elegant and wild. Everything he could never have or dare to be.

"Don't pity me," he said bitterly, unable to bear it from her. "I'm more than aware of who and what I am."

"You're ill at ease with large groups and people you are unfamiliar with," she said, refusing to be dissuaded from her topic of conversation. "You tell puns when you're nervous. That is all. Cease speaking as if you're some sort of monster, Neville."

He wasn't certain if it was her pointed use of his given name or the way she boiled his affliction down to something so mundane-sounding. Whatever the reason, he was suddenly beset by the urge to kiss her again. But that was foolish and most unwise.

"I *am* a monster." The coldhearted treatment he'd received had left him sure of it. "I was an unnatural child, an embarrassment to my family. My father wished I would have died in place of my younger brother Christopher, that the world would have been a better place for it."

His father's words would forever haunt him.

"You cannot believe that." Charity looked aghast at the suggestion.

He laughed without mirth. "Of course I can, my dear. He told me so with alarming regularity. Often as he was beating me."

He hadn't meant to reveal the last. And he knew he shouldn't have the moment her countenance shifted. Her lips parted, an undeniable expression of horror on her face.

"Forgive me for my bluntness," he bit out, shaking her hand from his sleeve. "As you can see, I'm hardly fit company in the best of moments and most definitely not at the worst. If you'll excuse me—"

"No." She moved swiftly, blocking him on the path, arms stretched wide on either side of her, as if she truly believed she possessed the superior strength to keep him anywhere he didn't wish to be. "Don't go. Talk to me, Neville. Please."

"There's nothing to talk about. I've warned you away from me. You had best take heed."

He wanted to pass by her. To stride deeper into the maze. But she remained stubborn in her determination, and he had no wish to bowl her over.

"I won't take heed," she told him firmly. "Stop trying to run away from me and listen, if you please."

"You can't say anything that will make this go away. I am who I am."

"Neville," she protested.

"Damn you, Charity," he snarled, feeling beastly.

When he'd been a lad, he had fallen from a cart when the horse had spooked. He'd held tenaciously on to the reins and been dragged along a rocky road for his efforts, until the knees of his trousers had torn away and he'd been left raw and bloodied. That was how he felt now in this moment with her, scraped and revealed and sore.

"There's nothing wrong with you," she exclaimed, flattening her palms against his chest.

He wondered if she could feel how fast his heart was pounding. He hated her touch, and he yearned for it. Wanted to haul her close and push her away.

"Everything is wrong with me," he countered harshly. "Otherwise, I wouldn't be so tempted to do this."

Without another word, without another thought, he lowered his head and took her lips with his.

CHAPTER 6

*H*is mouth came crashing down on hers.

Their hats were in the way, the brims knocking together. She tore at the ribbons holding hers in place and swept it from her head to the gravel path, not wanting any encumbrance to distract her. In almost the same breath, Neville whipped his hat away, tossing it to the ground.

Charity hadn't expected the ferociousness of his response. But now that she had his mouth on hers, she welcomed it. Welcomed *him*. Because his kisses had been all she'd been able to think about since earlier in the library. All through the painstaking process of pretending to enjoy herself whilst playing forfeits, and then through the early rounds of charades. She'd been sneaking glances in his direction, and the instant she'd seen him slip from the drawing room, she hadn't hesitated. With a bland excuse for Madeline and Lucy, she'd rushed from the chamber with all haste, intent upon catching him before he could retreat.

And she had him now.

Or rather, he had her.

Her heart ached for him, for what he must have endured at the hands of his father. And her body ached for him too. Her breasts felt heavy and painfully sensitive, trapped within the confines of her corset. Her nipples were hard and tight. Liquid heat pooled low in her belly. And the pulse between her legs was too much to ignore.

She'd read about these forbidden longings in the naughty books she'd managed to acquire without her parents knowing. But she'd never experienced it before. Not like this.

His hand cupped her nape, angling her head so that he could deepen the kiss. He parted her lips with his tongue, delving into her mouth, stroking and teasing and claiming. Setting her aflame. There was no chance of feeling the chill in the air this dreary afternoon. Because what she felt for Neville was a blazing fire, and it could only be extinguished in one way.

She wanted him to be her lover.

The astonishing thought pierced her feverish mind, a realization that shocked her. She wanted to know him. Wanted him in her bed, inside her body. The knowledge made her tremble.

He withdrew instantly, tearing his mouth from hers to frown down at her. "You're cold."

"No," she hastened to reassure him. "I'm burning."

"Charity." He was stern again, as if he'd somehow managed to summon all the control that had fled him the moment he'd kissed her with such wild abandon.

But she wasn't ready for him to return to his staid self. Not when she had him like this, so thoroughly undone. Her heart still ached for him. She wanted to show him that there was absolutely nothing wrong with the man he was. That she wanted him. She had watched him enough throughout the house party thus far to understand he was a good man, a kind man. He doted over his niece. He cared very much about Margaret's future. So much that he'd braved attending a house party that must have felt like torture to him. So much that he'd faced the demons of his past to bring her here. And Charity admired him for that and so much more.

"Don't try to dissuade me," she told him. "I know what I feel."

His lips rolled inward, and he took a long, slow inhalation, as if he were trying to calm himself and gather his thoughts. He hadn't released her or pushed her away, but his bearing had stiffened.

"There's nothing wrong with you," she repeated firmly, hoping that if she said it enough, he might believe her.

That she might undo some of the damage that had been done to him. Even if it was only a small amount.

"You needn't try to placate me." He stared at a place over her shoulder. "I don't want your pity."

Frustrated, she cupped his face in her hands, moving it gently so that he was forced to meet her gaze. "Does it look like pity on my face?"

His pale-green eyes devoured her, lingering overly long on her lips. "This is a mistake. I don't dare to allow things to progress any further than they already have. We should both return to the drawing room."

But she had no intention of surrendering that easily.

"Is that what you always do?" she pressed. "What you *should*?"

Viscount Wilton—Neville—stared down at her, looking as if he were at war with himself. He was smoldering with barely leashed desire, and yet his icy reserve was present too, along with all the ghosts of his past. He remained silent, but the hand he'd settled on the small of her back somehow during their passionate kiss increased its pressure, drawing her into him. The gesture was perhaps instinctive. She couldn't say. All she knew was that he didn't want to let her go any more than she wanted to release him.

She had no notion of what it was between them, this raging, passionate fire. But she wasn't ready for it to end. Not now. Not yet.

"Be brazen with me, Neville," she dared him. "You just may find you like it."

He muttered something beneath his breath that sounded suspiciously like an oath. "You don't know what you're asking of me."

He sounded torn. But he deserved to be free of the ties of duty and obligation. Even if only for a few fleeting moments. She knew what it had been like, weighed down by the trappings of polite society. By rules and propriety and the stinging censure directed at her after the rumor had begun to spread about *Venus at Her Bath*.

"The choice is yours." Extricating herself from his hold, she turned away, leaving him and their abandoned hats on the path, walking deeper into the maze, hoping he would follow.

Terrified he wouldn't.

She turned a corner, and suddenly, he was there, taking her back into his arms in a crushing embrace. Tall and strong and passionate as he crowded her into the boxwoods at her back and pressed his lips to hers. The kiss was voracious. Charity wrapped her arms around his neck, clinging to him, her lips moving with his. He made a low sound of need, as if he were helpless to do anything but give in to the passion between them. And she knew an answering sense of helpless desire. She opened for him, their tongues tangling, their breaths mingling, and she didn't care that her silk bustle crushed into the damp hedgerow at her back. She didn't care that the foliage of the boxwood caught in her chignon, unraveling her lady's maid's careful efforts of earlier.

She didn't care that at any moment, someone could round the corner in the maze and see them wrapped in each other's arms.

All she cared about was Neville, the devastatingly handsome viscount who was so much more than his stern façade hid. He kissed her until she forgot everything around them. Her entire world was comprised of his mouth angling over hers, his tongue sliding sinuously inside, his hard chest crushing into her breasts. He surrounded her, enveloped her, and she never wanted it to end. Never wanted him to move his lips from hers.

But when he did, dragging his mouth along her jaw, all the way to her ear, she offered no protest. Only a breathy moan. Her eyes fluttered closed and her head tipped back, deeper into the boxwoods, their fragrant aroma mingling with his woodsy, citrus scent.

"What have you done to me?" he whispered into her ear, his breath falling like hot velvet over her throat.

It was part demand, part frustrated question.

Her eyes still closed to blot out the gray sky and everything that wasn't him, she murmured, "Whatever it is, you've done the same to me."

"You've bewitched me." He nuzzled the hollow behind her ear, then rubbed his cheek against hers, the prickle of his shaved morning whiskers a delightful abrasion on her skin.

Had she? If so, she ought to be pleased with herself. Because she'd never experienced anything like what she felt now, in this man's powerful arms. It was as if he somehow saw past her, saw through her, saw her for who she truly was instead of the scandal every other man saw when he looked at her. And in return, she saw him.

And she liked what she saw.

"Ah God, Charity." Her name was a ragged groan in his low, deep voice.

In her impractical silk pumps, her toes curled.

His name fell from her lips, a whisper, a plea. "Neville."

She wanted... Heavens, she didn't even *know* what she wanted. All the sinful stories she'd read in her naughty books wove together into a vague blur that paled in comparison to the full effect of this man kissing her, leaning into her with the weight of his lean, muscled strength. She was a willing captive, trapped between Neville and the boxwood hedge, its smartly trimmed branches firm at her back, catching silk and likely making a ruin of her gown.

He kissed along her neck as he'd done in the library, following her throat until he found the curve of her shoulder. His mouth was open, hot, and she was panting, the knot of desire deep within her tightening to almost painful precision. His lips trailed along the edge of her bodice, teasing a slow path over first one breast, then the other.

The bodice of her gown fastened at the front. He pressed his lips to the space between her breasts, and she rubbed her cheek against his golden head, his soft hair a whisper on her skin that made her nipples ache. His fingers found the line of buttons bisecting silk and, without hesitation, plucked first one free and then the next and the next. Then the rest, almost down to her waist. He didn't stop until her bodice sagged in two halves, revealing her corset and chemise beneath.

He lifted his head, his lips leaving her bare skin, but remained intent upon the action of his hands as they swept over her breasts, cupping them. She arched into him, gasping, seeking. Neville's fingers hooked in her chemise and corset, just where her breasts threatened to spill from the top. With one firm tug, he freed them, dragging her corset low so that they were presented to him, bare, right there in the garden maze where anyone could happen upon them.

It was so unlike him.

81

Heavens, it was unlike her.

But with a deep sound of approval, he lowered his head and took the peak of her breast in his mouth, and she no longer cared. He sucked, and she gasped at the sheer pleasure of it, the vibrant sensation arcing through her. Her fingers sank into his hair, sifting through the thick dark-gold strands, so smooth and silken.

"Oh," she gasped as his tongue flicked over the turgid bud.

He moved to her other breast, sucking and licking, and she thought she might swoon from the sheer pleasure of it.

She'd read about a man placing his mouth on a woman's breast before. And of course, she'd been intrigued by the notion. But nothing could have prepared her for the actual sensation. For the hot suction of his lips over the surprisingly sensitive peak of her breast. She wanted to capture this feeling and never forget. He circled the distended bud with his tongue in a tease that had her pressing herself against him in a desperate plea for more. Just when she thought she couldn't bear another moment, he'd take her in his mouth again.

On and on, he went, torturing her, lavishing such attention on her breasts that she was no longer capable of rational thought. She was nothing but a quivering, panting being of pure, ravenous need. It was as if she had been made for him, made for this wicked tryst in the Sherborne Manor garden maze. And she never wanted it to end.

"You're so lovely," he praised, pressing a kiss to the swell of one breast, his hand molding and shaping the other, as if he couldn't touch her enough. "I want you so much I ache with it."

"Yes." She raked her fingers through his hair with firmer insistence, urging him on. "Please."

She wasn't even certain what she was pleading for. To take her, perhaps. To make her his in every sense of the word. And she knew what that meant. At least, she did in terms of what she'd read. But somehow, the explanations in her books, while intriguing and titillating, couldn't possibly compare to the way she felt.

"I can't." As if he'd been privy to her thoughts, Neville murmured the words against her bare skin. "Not like this."

Despite his words of denial, he fisted one of his hands in the voluminous fall of her silk skirts. He crushed it in his grasp, lifting it, sending the kiss of air over her ankle and calf as he dragged gown and petticoat and chemise higher. All the way to her waist. Using his hip, he pinned the fabric against her, leaving her limbs on display, nothing more than drawers and stockings to shield her. How strange and yet thrilling it was, to be so fully revealed to him and yet still wearing all her garments.

"God," he muttered, sounding frustrated with himself and torn. "What you do to me, sweet Charity."

No one had ever called her *sweet* before. Not even her former betrothed, nor any of the other gentlemen with whom she'd deigned to dally in darkened alcoves and inviting shadows since Ainsley had thrown her over. A kiss here or there, nothing more. Because she hadn't wanted anything more.

But this man had changed that.

Had changed everything she thought she knew about herself.

With a low growl of carnal need, he took her nipple in his mouth, suckling with greater urgency as his hand skimmed over the slit in her drawers. She couldn't look away from the incredibly erotic, wicked sight of his handsome face at her breasts. The knowledge that they could be interrupted at any second by a fellow houseguest only seemed to add to the thrill. She loved that she affected him so strongly. It was only fair, because he did the same to her.

She widened her stance, inviting him to touch her. To not stop at a mere brush against her undergarments. He needed no further nudging. His fingers unerringly glided inside the part in her drawers to skim over her heated flesh. The first touch of his bare hand on her most intimate place had her knees going weak.

Charity cried out as he traced up and down her folds, rubbing moisture that had gathered there into her sex. It felt so good, so wonderful. She couldn't contain herself, couldn't control her reaction to him.

He released the peak of her breast.

"Hush," he whispered. "Someone will hear you."

His mouth covered hers again. He fed her a kiss that was raw and sensual, his lips pressing into hers with passionate frenzy as his fingers boldly stroked her below, stoking the fires of her need ever higher. She felt as if she were wound as tightly as a spring, as if, at any moment, she would come free and shatter apart.

His tongue slid back inside her mouth, sweeping against hers, inciting a fresh, molten rush of greedy pleasure. Between her legs, he continued his insistent pressure, his clever fingers delving deeper until he found the sensitive knot of desire hidden there. She moaned into his kiss, and he drank it up as if it were air, his hand never easing pressure on her. He pleasured her until her knees gave out, and there was nothing holding her up save his big body pinning her to the boxwood hedges.

She hooked her leg around his hip, granting him greater access, wanting more of everything he was doing to her. More of his kisses, more of his touch. And he gave her that. With his mouth, he swallowed her every sound. His touch swirled in a sinful caress over the center of her, the place where it felt as if she was so very alive.

More sounds fled her. Desperate noises.

"Mmm," she moaned, senseless.

Completely beyond any ability to control herself.

He didn't appear to mind. He worked his hand harder between them. Faster. She was so close to something tremendous happening. To reaching that august height that was only possible through lovemaking. She had touched herself before, had caressed herself to completion, but that had been different. This was uncontrollable. It was wild; it was forbidden. She could scarcely believe Viscount Wilton was the man pinning her here, visiting such unrestrained pleasure upon her.

And yet he was.

He *was*, and oh dear God, she was going to...

Charity threw her head back into the hedges, not caring about the way the clipped boughs caught at her hair and scratched her neck. She cried out his name as a wave of something terrible and dark and wonderful overwhelmed her. Until stars speckled her vision and her lungs seemed to freeze in her chest, and she thought for a stunning moment as jubilant bliss washed over her that she may have perished and gone to her ultimate reward.

The pleasure was intense, making her shudder and tremble. She bent backward into the hedge, chasing his hand with her hips, seeking to wring every bit of pleasure from him that she could. When the last of her pinnacle subsided, she was left breathless, halfway mired in the boxwood hedge, her ears ringing with the force of her body's reaction. Her heart pounded as if she had run the entire length of the maze.

Neville was there, his body a big, protective shield, his face buried in her throat. He traced his lips reverently over the madly racing pulse at the hollow of her neck. Suddenly, against her inner thigh, she was aware of him, of not just the coarseness of his tweed trousers but of something else—*him*.

A thick, long ridge jutting into her tender flesh that could only be one thing.

His manhood. Or, as her wicked books had sometimes called it, his *cock*. It was the part of him that was meant to be inside her. But he hadn't put himself inside her, hadn't made love to her fully. Instead, he had brought her unimaginable pleasure. Grateful and dizzied with the aftermath of her almost violent release, she kissed his hair.

He pressed one more kiss to her neck and then lifted his head, his unusual gaze glittering into hers, so intense that for a moment, she forgot to breathe. "I shouldn't have done that."

Not the words she wanted to hear when she was still so open to him, when his hand was yet covering her mound, his fingers gently strumming her sex, sending ripples of new desire through her.

"But you did," she managed to say. "And you liked it."

She held his gaze, daring him to disagree.

"Yes," he agreed slowly, looking rather like a man emerging from the depths of a dream. "I did. Heaven help me, I did. But that doesn't make it right."

His touch left her then, and she mourned the loss, the cool air on her skin before he stepped back, allowing the curtain of her skirts to fall between them. She was still partially embedded in the blasted hedge, her bodice undone, her breasts bare, her hair caught on branches, her breathing ragged. And meanwhile, Neville looked vexingly perfect, not even a golden lock of hair falling over his brow.

"Forgive me," he said.

She struggled with her corset, attempting to tug it back into place. But the tightlacing from her lady's maid that morning was devilishly persistent, and she hadn't the strength.

"God," Neville muttered darkly. "Allow me."

His fingers chased hers as he caught her lace-and-satin

corset and chemise, pulling both with superior strength. Her breasts slipped mercifully back inside the constraints, shielded from his view, though still as achy and tender as if his mouth were on her. Something about his calm, almost imperturbable, air nettled Charity. When his fingers moved to refasten the line of buttons on her bodice, she sought them.

"I'll do it," she said, painfully aware her hands were trembling, each button suddenly far more difficult to land in its mooring than ever before.

He stepped away and watched her with a hooded stare, though still shielding her with his large body, blotting out the hint of sun that was attempting to emerge from the gray clouds overhead. A bird soared past, its joyous call splitting the sudden silence that had fallen between them and making Charity jump. The rest of the world suddenly returned to her —and, with it, consequences. She was no longer adrift in a sea of pleasure and seduction.

Charity finished the final button and began struggling to free herself from the boxwood, but to no avail. The branches snagged her delicate silk with such tenacity, she feared one false move would tear her bodice to shreds. And then what would she do, walk back through the main hall with her chemise and corset on display? How would she explain her state to anyone who saw her?

Worse, what if Auntie Louise happened upon her? Her aunt could always read through Charity with shocking ease. Auntie Louise would take one look at her and know instantly that she had been engaged in something far more wicked than any of her previous scrapes. And Lord knew there had been many previous scrapes. None, however, like this. No man had ever been so bold, nor proceeded so far with her, blithely down the path to ruination.

But then, she was already ruined, wasn't she? Hadn't

Ainsley made certain of that by throwing her over at the height of the gossip surrounding the painting? She'd heard the whispers herself when no one thought she was near enough to overhear. Society already believed she'd been compromised beyond redemption. Her lack of serious suitors upheld that belief. Gentlemen were more than willing to dally with her, to kiss her in dark corners, but no one would court her seriously.

She'd told herself it didn't matter.

And yet for some unfathomable reason, she felt as if it did now. With Neville.

"We should return to the drawing room at once," he was saying, his brow furrowed, his tone heavy and troubled. "Separately, of course. We have no wish to make tongues wag."

"I would," she bit out, "were I not caught in this blasted hedge."

"Curse it," he muttered, striding forward, towering over her as he reached for her hair. "Hold still. You'll only make it worse if you keep thrashing about."

She'd hardly been thrashing, and she was of half a mind to tell him so, but his sudden proximity was having a damning effect upon her capacity for coherent speech. Once more, his scent wrapped around her, and her body yet hummed with the aftereffects of his knowing touch. He had brought her to such a stunning crescendo—and so well, too. It hadn't been the first time Viscount Wilton had given a woman pleasure, that much was certain. And why the knowledge caused a pang of jealousy deep within her, she didn't care to examine.

With calm, efficient motions and a grim countenance, he unhooked her hair from the branches that had snagged it. A few moments more, and he had her gown freed as well.

Taking her hands in his, he pulled her from the vegetation and back onto the gravel path.

"Thank you," she said, still feeling oddly breathless and warm all over, her body overtaken by a languid, almost delirious ease unlike anything she'd ever known.

Neville shook his head, still far too serious for a man who had just made her entire world turn upside down mere minutes before. "Don't thank me. It was my fault. I'm a base scoundrel to take advantage of you here in the midst of the outdoors, and where anyone could have overtaken us. My God, the damage to Margaret's reputation…"

He shuddered, allowing his words to trail off.

And another peculiar emotion overwhelmed her then, one that had nothing to do with pleasure at all. "Thank heavens nothing untoward will befall your niece as a result of our folly," she said coolly, secretly congratulating herself on her sangfroid, when inwardly, she felt as if she were falling apart.

He had nearly made love to her in the boxwood hedge, and his concern wasn't at all for Charity's reputation. Rather, it was for his niece's. She didn't know why she should feel so disappointed at the realization. Certainly, she shouldn't have been as surprised as she felt.

"I didn't mean to suggest she alone would have been affected," he hastened to add, perhaps understanding the ramifications of his words better than those of his actions.

But it was too late. What had been said could not be unspoken. He couldn't take it back any more than she could pretend to herself that it didn't hurt. Because while the rest of society—those who didn't know her—might think her irredeemably ruined, that knowledge had never felt like a blow to her midsection the way it did now.

She forced a smile for his benefit. He may have just given

her the most incredible experience of her life, but he had also quickly tarnished it.

"Of course you did," she told him, holding his stare defiantly. "Why should anyone trouble themselves with my reputation when I'm already too scandalous to marry?"

She couldn't keep the bitterness from her voice. Before she said anything else she would regret later, she rushed past him, rounding the bend in the maze as he called after her. Charity only paused long enough to retrieve her hastily discarded hat, still on its top in the gravel, the silk ribbons adorning it lying in a rain puddle she hadn't taken note of earlier.

Her hat, just like her reputation, was ruined. How suiting. Charity jammed it onto her head, wishing for the day when that knowledge would no longer affect her.

"Charity."

Neville's long-limbed strides were eating up the distance between them.

But it was too late. Grasping handfuls of her gown to ease her escape, Charity fled from him, from the gardens, and from the reminder that she was not nearly as unaffected by the gossip surrounding her as she pretended.

CHAPTER 7

*H*e'd bollixed everything up.

Neville stared morosely at his glass of port, thinking about Charity's wounded expression when she'd fled him that afternoon in the maze. She'd ignored him through dinner, making certain she was seated at the opposite end of the table, studiously avoiding his gaze. And Lord knew he'd tried to catch her eye. He'd failed. And he'd subsequently muddled through a laborious, painful dinner in damning silence. Not even Margaret had wanted to converse with him, directing her attention to one of the younger gentlemen in attendance instead.

He couldn't blame her.

Couldn't blame Charity either.

It would seem that, over the last few days, he had let down both of them, and now he was paying the price.

"Ye're looking Friday-faced, my lord."

The observation, issued in a soft Scots burr, jolted Neville from his grim ruminations and self-castigation.

Neville glanced up from his untouched port to see Mr. Lachlan Macfie folding his massive frame into a chair at his side. Although he and Macfie were new acquaintances, having just met at the beginning of the house party, Neville found the man infinitely likable. He was a trusted friend of notoriously wealthy businessman Elijah Decker, who was also in attendance with his wife, leading light of the Lady's Suffrage Society, Lady Josephine Decker.

"The face matches the mood," he muttered darkly.

"Aye, I reckoned as much." Macfie nodded sagely. "A lass?"

"Two lasses." Neville sighed, knowing he shouldn't delve into further detail and yet wanting to unburden himself despite the fact that they were seated in the drawing room surrounded by a host of others.

Not a place where he ordinarily felt comfortable, to be sure.

"Would one of them be yer wee niece, Miss Astley?" Macfie asked politely.

Margaret was tall for a lady; impressive height was an Astley family trait. However, to a man of Macfie's tremendous size, perhaps everyone and everything else did seem small.

"She is one of them, yes," Neville conceded. "I'm afraid she is rather cross with me after I refused to allow her to go traipsing about the Continent largely unchaperoned at an indeterminate time in the future."

Which was every bit as ludicrous as it sounded. Ridiculousness seemed to be a hallmark of anything involving Lady Charity Manners. And lust. But he wouldn't think about that just now. Or, God willing, ever again. He couldn't afford to be attracted to her, let alone act on that magnetic draw any more than he already had.

"An excellent decision on yer part," Macfie said. "I cannae blame ye for that. And the lass will realize ye're only protecting her one day, even if she doesnae appreciate it now."

He wished he could be as sagely reassured about Margaret's ire. And his abilities as her guardian.

"The truth is, I haven't the slightest inkling of what to do with a twenty-year-old lady," he admitted. "I've never been a father myself. My brother and his wife died suddenly last year, and with Margaret unmarried and no other close family relations, I've been shouldering the responsibility of her return to the social whirl following her period of mourning."

And it wasn't going well.

Perhaps it would have gone better had he never seen Lady Charity Manners emerging from the lake two days ago. Or if he had never met her at all. But no, that notion left a strange, hollow feeling inside his chest.

"Ye're a good man," Macfie pronounced. "It cannae be easy, what ye're doing."

He didn't feel particularly good at the moment. After what had happened, his complete loss of control in the gardens earlier, he felt distinctly beastly.

Neville sighed heavily. "It's one of the most difficult tasks I've ever undertaken."

And not just because he detested polite society and all its trappings. But because he was a man, by God. He hadn't an inkling what young ladies liked. What interested them. What she'd want for her own future, as Charity had defiantly pointed out.

"I ken how difficult the burden of responsibility can be, particularly with a headstrong lass." Macfie raised his glass of port in salute. "The fairer sex in general is a damned difficult lot."

Neville thought he heard an undercurrent of something more than mere commiseration in the Scotsman's voice. "You're having a difficult time as well, then?"

"Aye. When am I no' having a difficult time?" Macfie

brought his glass to his lips, taking a small sip of the port before grimacing. "Dinnae tell our host, but I've never cared for port. Give me a good, bracing Scots whisky any day over this swill."

Neville chuckled. "I'm excellent at keeping secrets."

And that was because he ordinarily kept to himself. There wasn't anyone to divulge a confidence to when he was alone as he preferred, isolated in the country.

"Good man." Macfie thumped him on the back with one of his massive paws, using more force than necessary.

As luck would have it, Neville had been just about to take a sip of his own port. The rich, dark wine flew out of his glass, splashing over his hand.

"Ah, damn me." Macfie whipped a handkerchief from his coat and offered it to Neville. "Never did know my own strength."

The Scot was a brawny, roughhewn fellow. Friendly and pleasant, with a full head of red-gold hair and an ever-ready smile. He was also roughly the size of two men combined. He looked as if he could tear a chap apart with his bare hands and scarcely employ any effort.

"Think nothing of it." Neville patted at the spill, mopping it up with hasty motions. "It was my own lack of grace that caused it."

And God knew that was the truth, whether he was being thwacked on the back by a colossal Scot or not.

"Ye said two," Macfie said when Neville had finished cleaning up the port.

What the devil was the man talking about now?

Neville glanced back at the Scot. "I beg your pardon?"

"Ye said *two* lasses were causing ye to look as if someone pissed in yer soup course," Macfie elaborated. "But ye only mentioned just the one, yer wee niece."

Neville found himself absurdly tempted to laugh at the

Scot's blunt description. Would have, had he not been reminded of his folly in mentioning Charity to the man, even if not by name.

"The second is a far more complicated matter," he managed grimly. "I'll see your handkerchief laundered for you."

Macfie waved a hand dismissively. "Eh, think nothing of it. I've another dozen tae replace it. I leave the blasted things everywhere, ye ken, on account of always making messes." He frowned, as if troubled by something, before continuing. "Some more difficult tae clean than others."

"I know the feeling." Neville tucked the soiled handkerchief away, still fully intending to see it cleaned and returned to the Scot. "It seems I'm forever leaving a disaster in my wake. It's why I prefer solitude and the countryside to society."

And his latest mess had been nearly ravishing Lady Charity Manners in the maze in the midst of the day while a drawing room full of guests played happily at charades not far away. Where anyone could have come upon them, from gardener to gossip. He could have ruined her. And in so doing, he could have ruined Margaret's chances for a good match as well. To say nothing of his own.

He had made a terrible mistake. More than one, actually. First, he never should have allowed himself to be alone in Charity's presence after what had happened in the library. He ought to have known better, should have understood that his restraint had already been worn perilously low by her kisses. Second, he never should have kissed her again, nor done any of the rest.

But third, and worst of all, he had hurt her. He'd been half out of his mind, his body roaring with uncontrollable lust after having brought her to orgasm, the slick heat of her sex and her feverish response almost bringing him to his knees.

His cock had been painfully hard. His mind jumbled. And he had blurted out his concern for Margaret's reputation first, as if he didn't give a damn about Charity's. As if her reputation wasn't worthy of concern.

"Are ye going tae tell me who the second lass is?" Macfie asked, interrupting Neville's whirling thoughts.

"Are you going to tell me which lass is troubling you?" Neville countered, suspecting he already knew the answer.

Macfie raised a brow. "And what makes ye think that's what's troubling me? As my dear mother always said, ye never can tell what ails a man until ye've walked in his boots."

Neville chuckled. "I sincerely doubt your boots would fit me."

Not if the man's feet were as large as the rest of him. And that was a testament to the Scot's massive size, because Neville was a tall man himself, and of a muscular build from all the laboring he did on his country estate. Lachlan Macfie, however, would make a giant seem small by comparison.

"Ye ken what they say about boots, don't ye?" Macfie asked with a conspiratorial air.

Neville stared at the man. Surely he wasn't going to say something crude. Was he?

"I'm afraid not," he said, at a loss and just narrowly refraining from blurting a pun.

"The bigger the boots, the bigger the man's—"

"Mr. Macfie," Neville interrupted, not wanting to hear about the Scot's endowment. Or to think about it.

Ever.

"Feet," Macfie finished, giving him the devil's own grin. "What did ye think I was going tae say?"

Neville took up his glass of port and drained a few sips to avoid giving an answer, garnering him time to collect himself. "I'm sure I don't know," he muttered at last when he'd swallowed.

Not any more than he knew what to do about the sudden, inconvenient yearning burning deep inside him for one woman who was wholly wrong for him in every way.

"Och, ye're an easy one tae rile. Almost as easy as Decker." Macfie chuckled and gave Neville another thump on the back, this one a bit more subdued. "I like ye, Wilton. Ye're a stiff and proper one, but ye've a good heart beating in yer chest."

Neville wasn't sure if that was a compliment or an insult.

"Thank you, Mr. Macfie."

"Ye needn't thank me. But if ye wouldnae mind putting in a good word with Miss Madeline Chartrand on my behalf through yer lass, Lady Charity, I'd be grateful."

The Scot's words shocked Neville. Was he that obvious? Good heavens, he hoped not. He thought he had been rather circumspect with his interest. Until earlier today and his folly in the gardens, that was. But there had been no witnesses to his errant ways. He'd made certain no one else was about in the gardens when he had made his escape in the wake of Charity's retreat.

And further, he'd had no inclination that Macfie was interested in Miss Chartrand. She was one of the immensely wealthy American heiresses, a chum of Charity's.

"She's not *my* Lady Charity," he managed crisply.

"If ye say so," Macfie told him mildly.

"I *do* say so."

He clenched his jaw, thinking about how impossibly gorgeous she had looked after her morning swim, and about how she had been easily a hundred times more glorious in the maze, in a shocking state of *dishabille*. Flushed with desire he had caused, her bountiful breasts on display, all creamy and perfect and topped with hard pink nipples, more beautiful than any flower in the impressive Sherborne Manor gardens.

Sweet Christ, he had to stop this madness. He couldn't continue thinking about the wicked interlude in the maze. Or Lady Charity Manners at all. He needed to keep his distance from her. If Macfie suspected something was amiss between himself and Charity, then there was a good chance others did as well. And if others suspected something untoward was afoot, then it could well prove disastrous for Margaret. Particularly if anyone discovered what had happened between himself and Charity in the maze.

"My sainted mother had a favorite saying in such circumstances as these—methinks ye doth protest tae much," Macfie said agreeably.

"It would seem your mother borrowed it from Shakespeare's *Hamlet*," Neville couldn't help pointing out. "And she had it rather out of order. It should have been *the lady doth protest too much, methinks.*"

"Aye, but ye arenae a lady," Macfie said, his countenance hewn from stone.

A reluctant laugh left him. "Fair enough."

"My mother was a wise woman. But beyond that, she was the bonniest lass in all Scotland. How do ye think I came tae be so braw?"

Neville took a sip from his port to keep from chuckling again, for he couldn't tell if the Scot was in earnest or jesting, and he had no wish to insult the man. As large as Macfie was physically, his personality was easily twice the size.

"Now then," Macfie continued, undeterred, "let's return tae the favor I've asked of ye. I rather think Miss Chartrand doesnae hold any affection for me on account of my spilling champagne all over her puir dress the other evening. In my defense, the champagne tickled my nose. It was either sneeze all over the lass or try tae move out of the way. And as ye can imagine, a man of my size isnae always graceful. I moved quickly, and well, I spared her the sneeze but not, alas, the spill after all. Ruined the train of her fancy Paris silk, or so she told me."

Neville could only imagine the mountain of a man dumping champagne all over the American heiress's gown and her subsequent horror. Neville recalled the day their hostess and host had chosen a dance for the evening's entertainment all too well. He'd been horrified. He didn't dance, and the prospect of keeping an eye on Margaret in the whirling crush had nearly given him hives. He'd spent his time keeping company with a gathering of potted palms, his gaze straying from his niece to Charity, who had been vibrantly lovely in an evening gown of light-blue silk and pink roses.

God.

He had been watching her even then, drawn to her like a witless moth fluttering about a candle flame, unaware of his impending doom when his wings were inevitably singed. Only, he hadn't realized it until this very moment, how taken he'd been with her from the first occasion he'd seen her here. He had just entered the great hall after arriving with Margaret, and Charity had been laughing gaily with one of her friends. He'd been mesmerized by the sound.

By *her*.

Distance. That was what he needed. To make certain he spent the remainder of the house party as far from Lady Charity Manners as possible.

"Wilton? Are ye listening?" Macfie asked, jolting Neville from his whirling thoughts.

He blinked. "I am. Forgive me for woolgathering for a moment."

"Then ye agree?"

What was he agreeing to? Neville could ask, but then he would be admitting he'd lied just now when he had said he was listening.

"Of course," he said easily.

"Excellent man." Macfie thumped him on the back for a third time. "A picnic tomorrow afternoon for the four of us, then. I'll see tae the food. All ye have tae do is convince the ladies tae accompany us."

"The four of us?" he asked weakly.

The Scot beamed. "Ye, me, Lady Charity, and Miss Chartrand, of course. Och, and yer wee niece as well. Five of us, then."

A picnic with Charity tomorrow?

Neville drained the rest of his port. At least Margaret would be present. He would simply converse with his niece and pretend as if Charity wasn't even there. Surely he could survive one picnic with his restraint and his honor intact.

Couldn't he?

∿

THERE WAS something to be said for a gentleman in country tweed. Charity lifted her promenade dress to a discreet height as her sensible walking boots carried her over the rolling hills of the Sherborne Manor park, trying not to admire the masculine form directly before her and failing.

She didn't know how she'd allowed herself to be cozened into joining Neville, Mr. Macfie, and Madeline on a picnic lunch. All she did know was that the idea had been bandied about at breakfast, and now she found herself following the two gentlemen to their unknown destination, her friend Madeline at her side.

Miss Astley, Margaret, was meant to have accompanied them, but she withdrew at the last minute, pleading a headache and the need for a nap. Her absence meant that it was just the four of them—the huge Scot, the man Charity couldn't stop thinking about despite all her best intentions, a vexed-looking Madeline, and a resigned Charity. Something was simmering between Madeline and the tall, brawny Scotsman. Charity would bet her best hat on it.

"Why didn't you tell me *he* was coming along?" Madeline grumbled quietly at Charity's side.

"Lord Wilton?" Charity asked brightly, intentionally misunderstanding her friend. "I thought you knew he would be joining us when his niece suggested the picnic."

Madeline pursed her lips. "Not the viscount. The mountain."

Charity bit her lip to stifle a chuckle at her friend's uncharitable description of the burly Scot. "Mr. Macfie, you mean?"

Mr. Macfie cast a glance over his shoulder. "Aye? Ye need me for something, lassies?"

He was carrying a large picnic hamper that must have been heavy, and yet he carted it as if it were lighter than a feather. Neville had a counterpane tucked under one arm. The absence of servants, particularly given the length of their jaunt thus far, had been a surprise to Charity. As much of a surprise as Margaret's absence had been.

"Nothing at all, Mr. Macfie," Charity reassured him with a bright smile.

"How much farther will we be walking?" Madeline asked with a scowl. "We ought to be in Scotland by now."

"We're almost there," the Scot assured them with a wink and then continued on his way.

"We're almost there," Madeline muttered quietly, mimicking the Scottish lilt that marked Mr. Macfie's words.

Quite poorly.

"I can't think it will be much longer," Charity offered hopefully.

For they had been walking a great distance. Perhaps not to the long-limbed men in front of them, but certainly to

Charity and Madeline, weighed down as they were by their gowns and other encumbrances that were solely the plight of women.

"Why did I decide to accompany you on this dreadful picnic?" Madeline asked with a huff. "My boots are scraping my heels, and I'm beginning to perspire. I don't like walking. Good heavens, I don't even like being out of doors all that much."

Charity couldn't be sure if it was the prolonged march the gentlemen had been leading them on or if it was the presence of Mr. Macfie himself that had Madeline at sixes and sevens. Perhaps a combination of both. Heaven knew Charity herself was rather ill at ease being in such proximity to Neville the day after their ignominious parting in the maze, when he had all but made love to her.

She had only agreed to this picnic because Margaret had suggested it to her at breakfast. And when they had assembled in the great hall, she'd been quite dismayed to find Margaret missing. Neville had been awaiting her there, studiously avoiding her gaze as he stood with Mr. Macfie. She and Madeline had arrived together, both equally perturbed at the unexpectedly intimate nature of their picnic. Two couples.

Well, there was an obvious solution to their current dilemma. If Madeline disliked Mr. Macfie, and if Charity was nettled with Neville, that meant that she and her friend would simply spend their time with the gentleman least likely to vex them.

"You can pair off with Ne—Lord Wilton," Charity corrected herself hastily, tamping down the sudden pang of displeasure at the thought of watching her friend chatting and perhaps even flirting with the viscount. "And I'll spend the picnic with Mr. Macfie."

"No," Madeline refused with surprising haste.

Charity's brows rose as she cocked her head to the side and studied her friend whilst they continued traipsing up the hillside. "No?"

Madeline caught her lower lip in her teeth, looking troubled. "All I meant to say is that won't be necessary, dear. Although I do thank you for being so willing to suffer Mr. Macfie on my behalf. I know you have eyes for Lord Wilton. I'd never dream of keeping you from him."

"Eyes for Lord Wilton?" she repeated, far too loudly.

Neville glanced over his shoulder at her, frowning and looking every bit as grim as a man about to attend a funeral. Was that how much he wanted to avoid her presence? And if so, why should the thought send a painful slice of hurt directly through her?

"Carry on, my lord," she called. "We were simply talking about how lovely the weather is."

"As you wish, Lady Charity," he said before continuing on, his long legs keeping up with Mr. Macfie's massive strides with remarkable aplomb.

"I don't have eyes for him," she reassured her friend, taking care to keep her voice lower this time. "I don't even like him."

Unfortunately for Charity, that assertion was a lie. Because she did like the handsome, golden-haired, pun-wielding viscount. She liked him far too much. Which meant he was dangerous. Because she had no intention of allowing herself to be vulnerable for a man ever again. All she wanted was to enjoy this house party and then go to the Continent with Auntie Louise as they had planned.

"Truly?" Madeline asked with an arch look. "You don't look at him as if you don't like him."

"How do I look at him, then?" she asked, feeling unaccountably peevish.

"As if you want him to devour you."

103

Charity promptly tripped over the hem of her gown. The toe of her boot caught in her skirts, and she knew a wild moment of panic, her arms flailing around clumsily, as she sought to keep upright. But it was no use. Like a felled log, she tumbled to the ground. Everything unfolded in a blur. The grass came up to meet her, and whilst her fall was not graceful, her landing was even worse. She bounced off the ground in a pile of skirts and petticoats, her hat jostled from her head, corset cutting into her sides.

Pain radiated through every part of her body to rival the humiliation.

"Charity!" Madeline's shocked cry reached her as if from afar.

She realized it was because her face was buried in the calf-high grasses Mr. Macfie and Neville had been trampling on their way to wherever the picnic was meant to be laid. She lifted her head to find her friend's shocked face hovering over her, lined with worry.

"My goodness, have you hurt anything?" she asked.

Her pride. Good heavens, she'd hurt that. It was nothing but dust at the moment. Aside from that, she rolled over and winced as fresh pain emanated up her right leg. She struggled her way into a seated position, realizing she had somehow managed to twist her ankle whilst falling, and the hands she used to brace her fall were scraped and dirty, her gloves shredded from the rocks and dirt hiding beneath all the grass blades.

"I fell," she said lamely.

The crashing thumps behind her told Charity that Mr. Macfie and Neville had either witnessed her humiliating fall or had heard Madeline's shocked cries and were now hastening back to investigate. If ever there had been an opportune moment for the earth to open like a great, gaping maw and swallow her whole, she felt certain it was now.

"I'll help you up," Madeline volunteered, sticking out a gloved hand.

"Nonsense, lass," Mr. Macfie said, shouldering his way past Madeline and offering Charity an enormous paw. "Lady Charity may have injured herself. Did ye hit yer heid?"

"I don't think I did," she managed.

Neville dropped to his knees at her other side, taking her hands gently in his. "What happened?"

Heat crept up her throat. The truth was too humiliating to reveal. She'd been distracted by Madeline's observation, which had been far too close to the mark. And then she'd stumbled and caught her boot in her own hems and gone tumbling down. But she couldn't admit that to him. Not when he had been studiously avoiding her gaze and acting as if what had happened between them in the maze yesterday had been nothing more than a feverish dream she'd had in the night.

"I tripped," she said miserably, trying to move her ankle and wincing.

"You're hurt." He frowned at her, his eyes flashing with an emotion she couldn't read. "You've ruined your gloves, and your palms are bleeding. What else have you injured?"

"My ankle," she admitted. "It feels as if I twisted it when I fell."

"Do you think you can stand?" he asked, gently rubbing his thumbs in calming circles over the uninjured parts of her palms.

"I...don't know." She moved it again, more pain shooting up her leg.

"I'll carry ye back tae the manor house, my lady," Mr. Macfie volunteered, his tone grim. "It's all my fault ye fell. I shouldnae have chosen a picnic spot so bluidy far away." He paused, then added, "Er, forgive me for my coarse language."

The house may as well have been an entire country away,

given the current state of Charity's ankle. But although she appreciated the offer, she didn't think even a man who possessed Mr. Macfie's tremendous brawn could carry her all that way.

"I can walk," she protested.

"I'll carry her," Neville said in the same instant.

She blinked. Neville was strong. Indeed, her recent investigations of his person had proven he was well-muscled. However, he was nowhere near as enormous as Mr. Macfie, and she had doubted the Scot's ability to carry her back to the manor house.

"You can't carry me all that way," she told him. "I'll break your back."

"Of course I can." His jaw tightened, and he held her gaze, his countenance a study in tenacity.

"Och, let me carry the lass," Mr. Macfie intruded, his tone gentle. "As I said, I'm tae blame for this entire disaster."

"It's hardly a disaster, and it's not your fault," Charity countered, hating the guilty expression on Mr. Macfie's face. "It was my own lack of grace that caused me to trip and fall. I can make it back to Sherborne Manor on my own. I'll tend to my bruises and be just fine by supper. The three of you carry on and enjoy your picnic."

"You'll do nothing of the sort." Neville remained impassive as he flicked a glance up to where Mr. Macfie hovered over them. "Macfie, you and Miss Chartrand can proceed with the picnic as planned. I'll carry Lady Charity back so that she can have her wounds tended to. A physician ought to be called for, I should think."

"I don't need a physician," she protested.

But everyone ignored her.

Neville and Mr. Macfie were too busy squaring off like a pair of prizefighters, each determined to carry her back to the main house. Madeline was standing off to the side, chewing on her lip and looking dismayed.

"We should all return tae the main house," Mr. Macfie was arguing. "The picnic can wait for another day."

"Nonsense," Neville said smoothly. "With all the rain we've had lately, there's no telling if you'll have another clear day before the house party is over. Lady Charity will be in excellent hands with me."

For some reason, his words made her think about his hands on her quite literally. And his mouth, too. Oh, the pleasure his wicked caresses had brought her. The memory was enough to chase some of her pain. But then she remembered what had happened after that passionate embrace, and her ardor dampened and the agony in her ankle returned.

"Would the two of you please cease speaking about me as if I can't hear you?" she demanded, struggling into a sitting position.

Neville, who was still holding her hands in his, pulled her with ease, so that the movement scarcely required any effort.

"Gentlemen can be so overbearing," Madeline said then, shaking her head. "*I* will accompany you back to the main house, Charity. You can lean on me."

If she weren't in such dreadful discomfort, Charity would have laughed, for it seemed she had three separate champions, each vying for the opportunity to escort her back to Sherborne Manor.

"I can manage on my own, although I do thank you all for your concern," she reassured everyone, wincing again as she tugged her hands away from Neville's tender grasp and planted them on the ground in an effort to help herself into a standing position.

"Curse it," Neville said in a rare show of temper. "Let me aid you in standing. You needn't be so stubborn."

"I'm accustomed to looking after myself," she told him

pointedly, reminded of the need to guard herself in his presence after the day before.

The last thing she needed, given her past with Ainsley, was to give any man the chance to hurt her again. And she'd been perilously close to doing so with the viscount. How dismaying to think that all the bittersweet lessons she'd learned at the hands of her former betrothed had been for naught. To think she was still every bit as swayed by her foolish yearnings as she had previously been.

"That may be the case," Neville said calmly, taking her wrists firmly but gently. "However, even those who are accustomed to looking after themselves occasionally require the help of others. This is one such time, madam."

She glared at him. "I will stand on my own."

Even if her ankle fell off.

"Let. Me. Help. You," he gritted.

They stared at each other, at an impasse, Neville so near that she thought for a wild moment that he might lower his head, press his lips to hers, and kiss her into agreement. But then she recalled that they weren't alone. That Mr. Macfie and Madeline loomed over them as well. And further, that she was still furious with the man who was so insistent upon coming to her rescue.

Where had his heroics been yesterday?

Finally, she sighed, relenting against her better judgment. But only because she didn't wish to flop about on the ground like a fish that had just been reeled from a lake. Getting up from the ground in her corset and layers was tedious enough without an injured ankle and painful hands to add to the misery. And at the moment, she wasn't certain her pride could withstand much more.

"Very well," she allowed. "You may help me."

He muttered something that sounded suspiciously like "stubborn wench."

She didn't have much time to think about it, however, when he hauled her to her feet with sudden and surprising strength. One swift tug, and she was standing, but the pain in her ankle had her sucking in a breath and making a low, inadvertent noise.

"You see?" He was grim and distractingly handsome, frowning at her so severely that she longed to set her lips to his and kiss away his irritation.

Despite all the reasons why she shouldn't.

"Thank you for your aid, my lord," she said formally, irritated with herself for her reaction to him.

For her weakness where Neville Astley, Viscount Wilton, was concerned.

"Can you put any weight on your right foot?" he asked in a no-nonsense tone.

Gingerly, she tried, an ache shooting up her leg in the process. "I can, yes."

"Likely no' a sprain, then, and thank sweet heavens above for that," Mr. Macfie intoned. "Are ye certain ye dinnae wish for me tae carry ye back, Lady Charity?"

"Certain," she repeated. "I can walk."

"We'll *all* accompany you back to the main house," Madeline said fretfully.

Charity looked at Mr. Macfie, the picnic hamper still clutched in one of his big hands. She'd seen the way he looked at her friend as well. And that same, strange urge to play matchmaker between them rose. Even if it meant she would have to endure more time alone with Neville and submit herself to all the temptations that inevitably entailed.

It was plain to see that her friend was attempting to avoid being alone with Mr. Macfie, but it was also quite apparent to Charity that Madeline was drawn to him. And whilst Clementine was decidedly the matchmaker of their set, Charity couldn't help but feel rather tempted to assume the role. She'd seen Madeline casting glances in the handsome Scot's direction when she thought no one had been looking more than once. Mr. Macfie, despite his burly form, was a consummate gentleman. She had no doubt that nothing untoward would occur between the two. Unless Madeline wished it to, that was.

And heaven knew there had been rather a lot of furtive romantic trysts happening at Sherborne Manor during the house party.

"I'll go with Lord Wilton," Charity decided. "You and Mr. Macfie proceed and enjoy your picnic."

"But, Charity," Madeline protested, casting a wide-eyed glance in the Scot's direction. "Surely you don't expect us to make merry while you're suffering."

"I'll survive." She summoned a smile for her friend's benefit. "I assure you, I've endured far worse than a few scrapes and a twisted ankle. I'll be fine in no time. You and Mr. Macfie should enjoy the day. As Lord Wilton said, you ought to take advantage of the sunshine whilst we still have it."

Madeline sputtered.

"If ye insist, Lady Charity," Mr. Macfie said, his tone solicitous.

"I do," she told him firmly, slanting a glance in Neville's direction. "Lord Wilton, lead the way if you please."

He offered her his arm, and she took it, trying not to delight in his masculine strength or his decadent scent. She could ignore the effect he had upon her for the duration of their walk back to the manor house, she told herself. And from then, she would simply make certain to avoid him for the remainder of the house party.

Yes, that was all she needed to do.

CHAPTER 8

*S*he was in pain.

Clenching his jaw, Neville slanted another glance toward Charity, noting her paleness and her compressed lips. Their hobbling progress hadn't taken them far—just enough so that the shallow rises and falls of the gently sloped land had rendered Miss Chartrand and Mr. Macfie no longer visible. A rolling field of grasses and wild flowers, edged by trees on the far end, separated them from the manor house that presided over the park in the distance. Only its towering rooftop line was detectable from their present position. They had quite a great deal of walking remaining until she reached the haven of a comfortable place to recline.

And he knew her pride was driving her, as was her innate tenacity, but he couldn't bear another moment of her suffering.

"Stop," he ordered curtly, staying their progress by halting.

"I don't need to rest," she protested instantly. "The

quicker we return to the house, the better. I do fear my ankle is beginning to swell in my boot."

"I'll carry you the rest of the way," he told her.

Her response was instant and vehement. "No. You'll do nothing of the sort, my lord."

Her return to formality told him, along with the stiffness of her bearing ever since they had set off earlier in the day, that she was angry with him. He hated being the source of her ire, and he couldn't blame her. Yesterday, he'd been the worst sort of scoundrel. He had taken advantage of the moment, overwhelmed by the intensity of his attraction to her, without a thought for the consequences. And then he'd been a cad afterward, saying the wrong things. Doing the wrong things.

But this wasn't about what had happened between them. It was about her being injured.

"I'm carrying you, whether you like it or not."

"Can you not see how far it is? In case you failed to notice, I'm hardly a slip of a girl. You'll never be able to carry me all the way back to the manor house from here."

She was right—she wasn't a slip of a girl. She was all womanly, curved and rounded where it mattered. And he wanted to feel all that delicious softness pressed against him. Beneath him.

He swallowed hard against a rising tide of lust he couldn't afford to indulge. She was injured, damn it. What was wrong with him?

"I assure you, I'm no stripling myself," Neville reassured her. "I'll carry you."

"Why must you insist on being so stubborn?"

He could ask her the same question, but he was weary of arguing, so he simply bent and scooped her into his arms. She shrieked at the suddenness of his actions, apparently not believing him capable of exerting his superior strength to keep her from her own idiocy. Her arms flew around his neck, her magnificent blue eyes wide, and for a moment, he could scarcely breathe for the rightness of her in his arms, close to him, his to protect.

"What do you think you're doing?" she demanded, outraged.

"Keeping you from doing further harm to yourself," he informed her, feeling as grim as he sounded.

Because he couldn't allow himself to think such unwanted thoughts about her. Lady Charity Manners was too bloody troublesome and complicated and thoroughly altogether wrong for him. She was stubborn and fiery and wild and rebellious. She swam in lakes and kissed with abandon and posed for paintings in the nude. She had allowed him to pleasure her in the gardens. She brought out the basest, most sinful, perilous part of him. A part he hadn't known existed. And he couldn't risk any more such reckless behavior. Couldn't indulge in his rampant desires where she was concerned, however potent and alluring they may be.

And above all, he couldn't allow her to indulge her pride, possibly doing greater harm to herself in the process. If anything, it was painfully plain to see that Lady Charity Manners had a dangerous habit of doing whatever she wanted, with complete disregard for the consequences. Her disturbingly lax chaperone may not have any control over her, but Neville was damned if he was going to allow her to hurt herself whilst he stood idly by and watched.

He started off at a determined pace, marching through the grass as if he were a soldier in an infantry brigade, set upon meeting his enemy and delivering a death blow.

"Lord Wilton," Charity said, sounding most aggrieved.

"Lady Charity," he returned agreeably, keeping his gaze toward the horizon and their inevitable destination.

She was his own personal Gorgon, and if he glanced

down at her, it was entirely possible he would lose his resolve.

"Put me down," she grumbled. "This is ridiculous. You're behaving abominably. I'll not be carted about as if I'm a sack of flour—and with a complete disregard for my own wishes."

"I'm more concerned with your welfare than your wishes at the moment."

But his response didn't appease her. Not that he'd expected it would.

She continued.

"This is the most high-handed, abominable, utterly—"

He silenced her the only way he knew how, by setting his mouth firmly on hers and kissing her. It wasn't a passionate kiss—he had no wish to drop her. Rather, it was a swift press of his lips to hers. Neville somehow managed it all without tripping or missing a stride.

He raised his head, and she was quiet. Her countenance was adorably befuddled, as if she couldn't comprehend what had just happened. Neville would have kissed her again, but he had no wish to trip over his own feet and send them both sprawling to the ground.

And now, he was looking at her. True to his fear, he was losing his resolve, but he was also finding it deuced hard to look away. To keep his eyes where they belonged—on the uneven path back to the manor house.

"You kissed me," she said, her tone accusing.

He bit his lip to keep from grinning like a fool. It was rare to hear her so flummoxed. He liked it.

"I did."

"I wasn't finished speaking."

"Oh?" He slanted a glance down at her because he couldn't resist, then flicked his gaze hastily back up. "And what was it you were saying, my lady?"

"I…" She faltered, clearly having forgotten.

Just as he'd thought.

They traveled on in silence until they reached the gathering of trees ringing the park. He was accustomed to a great deal of labor, and he'd built his muscles steadily over the years. Carrying her didn't even wind him. And it was fortunate, because his masculine dignity might have been in danger otherwise.

"I can walk on my own," she protested when they ventured into the shadows of the trees, where light filtered from the leafy boughs sparingly and the air was cool and earth-scented.

"But you're in pain."

"I've been in worse pain," she told him, "only it wasn't in my ankle."

"Where was it, then?" he asked, suspecting he knew the answer.

"My heart." She lifted her chin, then unwound one arm from around his neck and thumped on the brim of his hat with her forefinger for emphasis. "The man I was meant to marry believed the worst of me and threw me over instead of marrying me, and all over a silly scandal I could have explained had he but wished to listen. So, you see? This little injury to my ankle and pride is naught compared to what I've already endured."

Neville almost did trip then, but not because he wasn't paying attention to where he was walking. Rather, because he knew the scandal she was speaking of—the nude Venus painting. Also, because he wanted to punch the man she'd given her heart to. Hadn't he understood what a rare, beautiful gift he'd been given?

"Any man who threw you over wasn't worth the pain he caused," he said firmly, keeping his gaze averted. "Indeed, he wasn't worth a goddamn—and certainly not worthy of you."

He didn't curse often, but there was something extra

satisfying about the oath that left him now. It was as much directed toward her errant suitor as himself, because Neville was painfully aware of his own complicity in believing the worst of her, even if it had been internal and he hadn't had the opportunity to get to know the woman in his arms as thoroughly as he thought he knew her now.

Which was quite well, when it came to physical intimacy. However, he couldn't shake the feeling that there was a great deal she kept secret and locked away, a part of herself that had nothing to do with her body and her desire, but everything to do with the woman within. And it shocked him to realize he wanted to know her. Even if he shouldn't.

He most certainly, absolutely shouldn't.

"Do you know, Neville," she began thoughtfully, her use of his given name sending an unwanted arrow of lust straight to his groin even as he carried her through the trees. "I think that is one of the nicest things anyone has ever said to me."

Her words filled him with shameful warmth. He didn't know how to answer them. Didn't know what to say to her. For the first time, his vexing mind was even painfully bereft of a convenient pun. So in the end, he said nothing, carrying her stoically on to the manor house.

~

"LORD WILTON, thank you for carrying my darling niece all this way. You are to be commended for your gallantry."

Charity watched from her perch on a divan in Vivi's private sitting room while Auntie Louise fawned over Neville as if he had saved her from the terrifying grips of certain death, instead of carrying her across bucolic fields of grasses and wild flowers. Not that his effort hadn't been

Herculean. Charity remained suitably impressed with his ability to cart her for such a long distance whilst barely losing his breath and certainly never faltering. However, her aunt's effusive praise was rather hyperbolic.

After all, Charity had wanted to walk. She *would* have walked, had he not swept her into his strong arms as if he were some sort of medieval knight intent upon rescuing a fallen maiden. The notion made a chortle slip from her lips unintentionally. Yes, she had the fallen part correct. And never more so than now, after she had all but rolled about with the viscount in the garden maze as if she were a wanton country dairymaid begging for a tup.

That thought, far more than the rest, sobered her.

But Auntie Louise's light-blue eyes had already swung to her, along with Neville's searching gaze. The gaze that saw too much, slicing right to the heart of her. To the tender, vulnerable place she'd sworn no longer existed until a few days ago.

Until *him*.

"Is something amiss, dearest?" Auntie Louise asked, her face etched with concern.

"Is your injury paining you?" Neville queried in almost the same moment.

And this, too, might have been laughable, under any other circumstances. Here were her beloved aunt and Viscount Wilton, fussing over her in concert, as if she were an invalid who couldn't attend to herself. Neville's concern made her feel as if her corset was too tight. Which it undoubtedly was. But that was another matter. It also made her feel as if her neck and ears were on fire. And it made a strange sensation blossom deeper inside her. An inner warmth that was more disturbing than any of the rest.

"My dear, what is it?" Auntie Louise asked, swishing to

her side and patting her hand. "Do you need something while we wait for the physician to arrive? Shall I ring for some water? Some lemonade, perhaps?"

"Or something stronger?" Neville asked, hovering over her with a worried frown. "Would you prefer claret?"

He had carried her all the way to this room, hidden away from the rest of the houseguests, at Vivi's behest. Her dear friend had taken one look at the sight they must have presented—a bedraggled, scraped, and muddied Charity being held by a somber, determined Lord Wilton—and had ushered them into the private chamber. After sending for Auntie Louise, who had been happily distracted in the card room, Vivi had excused herself to make certain a doctor was fetched to examine Charity's ankle.

It was unnecessary, and Charity had protested as much, but Vivi and Neville had insisted. And then Vivi had slipped away, and Auntie Louise had arrived, fluttering over her in melodramatic fashion. And still, Neville remained, his concern for her almost palpable, affecting Charity in strange ways.

She wished he would go away. But she also wished he would stay. Wished the memory of his strong arms wrapped around her, his warmth seeping into her, and his delicious forest-and-citrus scent invading her senses would dissipate like the rain clouds of the day before. She wished she could keep that scent in a locket, open it and think of him when she was long gone to the Continent and her adventure with Auntie Louise, when he was nothing more than a memory.

"Charity, darling, speak to me," Auntie Louise begged. "It's not like you to be so silent."

"Claret," Neville said, as if she'd answered.

He strode from the room, not even bothering to ring for a servant. The door clicked closed, and she was alone with her aunt, who still lingered at her side with a pale, drawn countenance, her golden hair tamed into an elegant chignon at her nape. She was wearing a gown of peach silk faille, an ornate brooch clasped at her throat. She'd always been more like a mother to Charity than her own icily reserved mother had been. But then, Charity had sorely tested Mother's patience. She hadn't been like her siblings. She was the youngest, the wildest. Even before her scandal, she'd been wayward. Too loud, too bold, too happy, too undignified, too unmannerly. Only Auntie Louise had been patient with her.

Auntie Louise had always been there at her side when no one else had. When Charity's mean harridan of a governess, Miss Leigh, had rapped her knuckles with a wooden ruler for forgetting her comportment, Auntie Louise had been there to dry her tears and make certain Mother and Father gave the wretched woman the sack.

"Thank you," Charity blurted.

Auntie Louise pulled a gilt-backed chair nearer to the divan, the legs scraping across the Axminster in a soft sound. "You needn't thank me, my dear. Lord Wilton is the one who carried you all the way here. You ought to direct your gratitude toward him. My, what a strong young man, to carry you so far."

He *was* strong. Lean and muscled, too. Far stronger than she would have suspected. Not at all like an idle lord. Certainly nothing like Ainsley, who had been too dignified to do anything more than ride his horse down Rotten Row at the fashionable hour.

"Thank you for always being here for me when I find myself in a scrape," Charity elaborated, cognizant of the fact that she had never given voice to her appreciation for her aunt.

"This is hardly a scrape, darling." Auntie Louise patted her hand again. "You twisted your ankle. It wasn't your fault."

But it had been her fault. She'd been thinking about

Neville. Hadn't been taking care with her steps. Her boot had been caught in her own hems.

"Still," she insisted, "you're always here to dry my tears or offer your shoulder when I need it. I remember when I was a girl and I was so terribly ill with fever, and no one dared to come near me, not even Nurse. But you were there, holding me, stroking my hair."

Auntie Louise gave her a tender smile. "It was my duty and honor to be there, dear heart."

"You became ill yourself, afterward," she remembered, recalling when she'd been well enough to emerge from the sickroom, looking for her aunt, only to be told Auntie Louise was now abed. She'd been beside herself with worry until she'd been allowed to see her aunt again.

"It was worth it," Auntie Louise said simply.

"And my awful governess, do you remember her?" Charity continued.

"Miss Leigh." Her aunt's lip curled in undisguised disgust. "A heartless witch. I ought to have broken that ruler over her head."

Charity chuckled. "I rather wish you had."

Another pat to her hand, Auntie Louise's so similar to hers and yet marked by years, the blue veins standing in relief against her pale skin, the gold-and-sapphire ring she always wore winking from one of her fingers.

"So do I, darling girl. And more. She made my sweet Charity cry, and for what reason? Some people should not be given the power they wield over others, and that wretched governess was one."

"She was," Charity agreed. "You've always been my champion. Even through the scandal."

"That scandal ought to have never happened," Auntie Louise said grimly. "I've been thinking of ways I might have my revenge upon Lady Featherstone for the entirety of this house party. A well-timed push into the lake, an accidental overturning of a soup tureen into her lap, a spider in her undergarments..."

Charity couldn't help but laugh. "But where would you find the spider?"

"There has to be a convenient arachnid somewhere in residence," her aunt said.

"Now you sound like Edie. Have you been reading one of her scientific treatises?"

"Of course not. Look at me." Auntie Louise waved gaily toward her impeccable gown. "Do I look like I read scientific nonsense to you?"

She smiled. "You do know how to bring me cheer, Auntie."

"A solemn duty of mine." Her aunt nodded.

"After what happened with the painting..."

"Never mind what happened," Auntie Louise said firmly. "One can never trust a Richards, and I do hope you have learned your lesson."

Hmm.

Fancy that, Auntie Louise taking her to task. For all Charity's life, her aunt had been an omnipresent figure. Guiding, coaching, encouraging. Never judging. Forever praising. The judging had been her mother's and father's tasks. At least, so it had seemed. When one possessed siblings who were never at fault and who did their duty and made excellent matches with ease, all without ever once bringing shame upon the family, well, how could a lady with a mind and spirit of her own ever possibly compete?

She could not.

"Peter was an excellent chum when he was in leading strings and I in short skirts," she offered to Auntie Louise in defense of her old friend who was responsible for the Venus painting and ensuing scandal. "However, I concede that I should never have agreed to sit for the portrait."

"Sitting for the portrait was never the problem, dearest, and you know it," Auntie Louise said as she fussed with a tendril of hair that had fallen from Charity's coiffure. "It was the manner in which Mr. Richards portrayed you."

Mr. Richards. How formal. He had always been nothing other than Peter to Charity. But then, she and Peter had been friends for years. Rather in the fashion of brother and sister, even if they were nearly of an age.

Charity frowned at her beloved aunt. "I don't think Peter was portraying *me*. He is no different from a brother to me, and I most certainly have never *disrobed* before him."

"And yet the undeniable likeness was enough to cause tongues to wag," Auntie Louise pointed out, her tone calm and precise, if a bit grim. "He should have known better than to invite such unwelcome speculation. A few changes to your countenance, and the resemblance would have been much more easily dismissed. I'd like to box that young man's ears for the pain he brought upon you."

Again, Auntie Louise was correct in her assessment. Yet, Peter had been as naïve as Charity had been. She couldn't blame him for the damage his painting had caused to her reputation, especially considering what the painting had done for his hopes as an artist. Peter was exceptionally talented, and *Venus at Her Bath* had managed to achieve tremendous attention, albeit years after it had originally been painted. But whilst he had gained much because of the painting, Charity had lost everything.

The door to the sitting room clicked open, and Neville returned, bearing a glass of claret. "The physician should be here within the hour."

He was at Charity's side in a trice, offering her the glass.

She accepted, their fingers brushing, an arc of awareness singeing a path directly to her core. How was it that he made her feel so painfully alive, as if her entire body had been fashioned for his?

"Thank you," she managed past the longing stirring up again, trying not to think about how he had tended to the scrapes and dirt on her palms when they had first returned to the manor house.

Despite her protestations that she could wash her own hands perfectly well, naturally. And she had allowed him to, just as she had relented and let him carry her. Because being tended to felt good. Particularly when Neville was the one doing the tending.

He straightened, removing his hold on the glass as if her touch had burned him. "Take a sip. It will help to dull the pain until the doctor arrives."

For some reason, she listened to him, obeying as she brought the glass to her lips. The claret was smooth and cool on her tongue. She swallowed. But it wasn't the pain she was trying to dull. It was the way he made her feel.

Exposed like the raw flesh on her palms.

Seen in a way no one before him ever had.

And all while Auntie Louise watched on, a calm, imperturbable chaperone. Charity and Neville had known far greater intimacies than this moment. He had pleasured her, touched her, kissed her. Had bared her breasts and sucked her nipples. Despite that, this moment felt eerily more intimate than any of the scandalous interludes that had preceded it. Because her aunt was looking at her in a way that said she *knew*. She knew the way Wilton made Charity feel, all the way to her marrow.

"It was kind of you to fetch the claret," Auntie Louise told him, smiling indulgently.

Charity was grateful for her aunt's presence. She had

accompanied her to Sherborne Manor for the house party, just as she always accompanied Charity everywhere. Mother and Father were forever far too busy with Charity's older siblings and their own friends to have a care for her. But that was fine as far as Charity was concerned. She had always felt much closer to Auntie Louise than to her mother or her sister. Her aunt understood her in a way no one else had.

Until Neville.

Charity brought the glass to her lips and drank some more of the red wine to soothe her frayed spirits.

"Since I'm at fault for Lady Charity's current state, it was the least I could do, Lady Louise," Neville offered politely.

Charity wondered if he was speaking about more than her ankle. He had loosened her laces before Auntie Louise had bustled into the room and had carefully removed her boot. His long fingers had gently probed and prodded her tender ankle. And she had been caught between the pain caused by her injury and the pain caused by her aching heart, that foolish organ she'd thought long devoid of the ability to feel.

How wrong she'd been.

Somehow, during their walk back to the manor house, the pieces inside Charity had fallen into place. And she'd come to an astonishing realization that shocked even her.

She wanted Neville. One night. It was all she could allow herself. But before this house party reached its conclusion, she was going to give herself to him. After that, she would carry on with her planned travels. She and Auntie Louise would see the world.

"Nonsense, Lord Wilton," Auntie Louise was saying now, dragging Charity from the depths of her madly churning thoughts. "You're hardly to blame for her injury, and the gallant manner in which you carried her all the way back…

Well, suffice it to say that most gentlemen wouldn't be nearly so chivalrous."

It was a pointed barb, directly aimed at Ainsley if Charity had ever heard one. But for the first time since the earl's defection, thinking about him didn't fill her nearly as full of resentment and anger as it ordinarily had. No. Indeed, when she thought about him now, all she felt was a tranquil sense of acceptance. Even relief.

If he hadn't thrown her over, she would be a married woman by now. And if she had been a married woman when she met Viscount Wilton at this house party, she never would have kissed him. Never would have heard the painful secrets of his past. Never would have walked with him in the maze. Good heavens, she would have missed so much.

She would have missed everything.

Neville accepted her aunt's praise with the expected awkwardness, his high cheekbones tinged with red. "It's nothing, Lady Louise. Less than nothing. The least I could do, truly."

Charity half expected him to blurt a pun. Perhaps he would have had his discomfiture run any higher. As it was, she had begun to notice that the more time he spent in her presence, the fewer puns he blurted. Which meant, she reckoned, that he felt comfortable with her.

"We are grateful for your aid, are we not, Charity?" Auntie Louise prodded with a pointed look in her direction.

"Quite grateful," Charity said, her gaze finding Neville's and holding it.

She felt the connection there, and her irritation over his high-handedness dissipated beneath its scorching strength. Unspoken words lay between them. How strange it was that she felt as if she knew him, truly knew him, in a way she'd never come to understand another. And after such a short acquaintance. But it was there, simmering beneath the silent understanding, like a candle waiting to be lit.

A discreet knock at the door interrupted, severing the moment. It was Vivi, still looking concerned, leading a portly middle-aged man carrying a dark bag. The physician. Neville took his leave, and Charity watched him go, already plotting how she would persuade him to be reckless with her for one night only.

CHAPTER 9

Discovering which of the dozens of guest rooms in Sherborne Manor had been assigned to Neville had proven quite easy. Avoiding her fellow guests' notice as Charity stole through the halls, a pronounced limp hindering her stealthiness, hadn't been nearly as simple. But at last, here she was, ensconced in his bedroom, seated pleasantly in a wingback chair by the hearth, waiting for him.

Her ankle was throbbing; she'd borrowed one of his pillows and arranged a low table to prop it. While the doctor had proclaimed her injury a mere sprain, he'd also ordered her to remain abed for the next few days, placing as little weight on it as possible while she convalesced.

The moment Auntie Louise had left Charity alone, she'd been out of bed, hobbling around her room and making preparations. A sprained ankle wasn't going to keep her from what she wanted. And under no circumstances would Lady Charity Manners concede to remaining abed for days. Not when she had a house party with her friends to enjoy, and most certainly not when she had a viscount to seduce.

Which was what she was doing now, wearing her most revealing gown and almost nothing beneath it.

She had told her lady's maid she was going to sleep early this evening. She'd told Auntie Louise the same lie. Charity didn't like dishonesty of any sort. Ainsley had lied to her when he had told her that he loved her, only to abandon her at the slightest hint of trouble. She knew she should feel guilty for fibbing to her aunt, particularly after the worry she'd caused earlier and the way Auntie Louise had fussed over her, making certain that her favorite meal was sent up on a tray, sitting with her for two hours just to keep her company.

But Charity didn't feel guilty. She felt...elated. Anxious, too. There was a distinct chance that Neville's sense of propriety and duty would eclipse his desire for her. Coming to his chamber had been a risk. He could reject her. Her presence, should she be discovered, could tarnish his niece's reputation. And yet she'd come here anyway. Because something had changed while Neville had carried her all that way in his arms, and if she had learned anything from living in the aftermath of her own scandal, it was that she didn't want regret to eat away at her.

She didn't want to squander this chance. If she didn't take it now, it would be lost to her forever. And she couldn't bear that.

So she was here, in a room that smelled of oiled wood and leather and citrus with a hint of pine and the more comforting scent of the morning's fire still smoldering in the grate. Waiting for him.

The door opened as if she'd willed it, and suddenly, he was there at the threshold, filling the doorway with his broad shoulders and tall, elegant form. He was dressed in immaculate evening clothes, his golden hair glinting in the lamplight, his necktie and shirt both snowy white in stark contrast to his dark trousers and coat.

Their stares clashed, and she held her breath, waiting for his response, the force of their melding gazes like velvet and fire to her senses.

He said nothing, simply stood there holding her gaze, his bearing stiff, his face exquisitely beautiful. And then, as if pulled by the same inevitable magnetism drawing them together, he crossed the threshold, snapping the door closed at his back.

"Charity."

Her name. That was all.

But he said it like it was a wicked word. Like it was a forbidden sin and he couldn't wait to partake of it, even though he knew he shouldn't.

She forced a smile she didn't feel, summoning all the daring and confidence she possessed. "Hullo."

His long-legged strides ate up the distance separating them. "You're in my chamber."

"Yes."

"You can't be here."

"Why not? It's perfectly comfortable."

He stopped before her and surprised her by dropping to his knees on the Axminster. "You know why not."

Charity leaned forward, drinking in the sight of him, their faces perilously near to each other now, so close his breath was a curtain dropping over her eager lips. "No, I don't. Tell me."

"Because this is my bedroom." His head tipped forward, and he pressed his forehead to hers.

"That's why I'm here."

He knew it. So did she. This was what the last few days had been leading to, its inevitability written in stone. They wanted each other. Why shouldn't they seize this opportunity?

"What language should a linguist end with?" he murmured.

For a moment, she couldn't think of a single response. It took her a few seconds to realize he was using another pun. That he was nervous.

She grazed her lips over his gently, taking a swift, almost chaste kiss while she dared. "I don't know."

"Finnish," he said grimly.

And then he cupped her cheek with so much tenderness that she nearly melted, and he took her mouth in a kiss that was ferocious and demanding and coaxing all at once. It was everything she longed for from him and more. She was smiling into that kiss, she realized. Smiling because he hadn't told her to go, because he was kissing her. Because he tasted sweet like wine and Neville and wickedness, and his tongue slipped inside her mouth to tangle with hers, and he made a low, deep rumble of appreciation in his chest as if he'd been starved for her.

But just as quickly as he deepened the kiss, he reared back, tearing his mouth from hers, his gaze traveling over her face, searching. "Your ankle. How did you get here?"

"I walked." She turned her head, pressing a kiss to his hot palm. "Slowly."

"Blast it, woman. Have you no care for yourself?"

His frustrated growl made her smile more. His protectiveness pleased her, and she couldn't say why.

"I wanted to see you," she said simply, "and I knew you wouldn't come to me."

"Of course I wouldn't." He traced the periphery of her lower lip with his thumb, and it startled her to realize it was callused, as if from manual labor. "It wouldn't be proper."

The rasp of his work-roughened skin over her lip was

strangely rousing. Liquid heat pooled between her legs. Her ankle, propped as it was on the pillow, scarcely even pained her now.

"You should know by now that I'm hardly proper," she told him.

"Why are you here?" he asked, his pale-green eyes searing into hers.

She reached for him, unable to keep from touching him then, one hand sweeping a lock of hair from his forehead, the other settling on his necktie, tugging at the knot. "You know why."

"Charity."

This time, her name was less of a caress, more of a protest.

"Don't try to dissuade me," she said resolutely. "I know what I want."

"And what is that?"

"You." She glided her hand down his neck, to his shoulder, relishing the heat of his skin, the prickle of his shaven whiskers that glimmered golden. "I want you to finish what you started in the maze."

He closed his eyes and inhaled sharply, as if her words had caused him physical pain. When he opened them again, he held her stare, unflinching. "We aren't married."

"Nor are we going to be," she countered practically. "We needn't be, you know."

"But it isn't right, Charity. I would be dishonoring you."

She shook her head. "Not if I ask it of you. Not if I want it."

He sighed heavily. "And Margaret. If word were to travel that I acted as anything less than a gentleman here, it could affect her future."

"No one will know."

"*I'll* know." His countenance was stern and forbidding.

But he didn't fool her. The passion simmering between them was enough to scorch them both.

"Don't tell anyone else."

"But—"

She silenced him with a finger pressed to his lips. "Hush. I was very careful about coming here. No one saw me. Do you think I want another scandal?"

He kissed her finger, and a quivery sensation stole through her at the contact. "I think you're still suffering from the first one."

He was correct. Or, at least, he had been. Because Charity knew what she felt right now, and suffering had nothing to do with it. Indeed, Ainsley was far from her mind.

"Anyone who believes I posed nude for that painting can go to the devil," she said.

Something in his expression changed. She saw it instantly and knew the reason.

"I have a confession to make," he said, sounding uneasy.

Her stomach flipped. "I'd rather you didn't."

She didn't want to hear it.

He sighed, holding her gaze. "Before I knew you, I believed the rumor. The resemblance to you is quite strong. I'm sorry, Charity. I shouldn't have believed it."

It was Charity's turn to sigh now. "The resemblance is strong because it *is* me. I did sit for the painting, but I was fully clothed. It was only later, after Peter wrote to me that it was on display at the Grosvenor Gallery, begging my forgiveness, that I realized what he'd done."

Neville stiffened, his jaw tightening. "He dared to paint you that way without your permission?"

She hadn't thought about it that way until now. Peter was a friend. His father was a baron, and his family lived on the estate bordering her father's country seat. They had played together as children. His elder sister had married her brother. And then one day, Peter had asked her to sit for a sketch. She'd done so, thinking it a passing fancy. She'd been eighteen, newly come out, unaware of the danger lurking in society's waters, just waiting for her to wade in. Charity had forgotten about the sketch until the whispers had started. At first, she had ignored them. Until Peter's letter had arrived. And then, she'd gone to see the painting herself.

By then, the gossip had raged through London to rival the Great Fire.

"It was a sketch," she explained. "We've known each other since we were children. I scarcely thought anything of it. Had I known he intended to paint me, and without a single stitch, I wouldn't have allowed it. But by the time I understood there was a Venus on display bearing my image, it was already too late."

"What did your family do?" Neville demanded.

"Why should they do anything?"

"Because you're their daughter, their sister, damn it. You say the artist was a family friend. Surely your family would have come to your defense."

Charity sat back in her chair, stunned by his vehemence, but also by his words. "They didn't."

Because, in hindsight, it was entirely possible her family had believed it too. She was the wild and wayward child, the hoyden, the disaster, the breaker of rules, the loud one who never seated herself with her spine straight enough. The scandal.

"They should have, damn their hides." He was still cupping her cheek, but now his thumb had moved again, traveling along her cheekbone in slow, soothing strokes that were at odds with the anger in his voice. "Do you know what your problem is, Lady Charity Manners?"

That she had never fit into the mold her family and polite society had made for her.

That she was falling dangerously hard for an unattainable viscount.

That she was the sort of lady who stole into a gentleman's bedroom at a country house party and swam in her chemise in the lake and allowed a man to kiss her witless in the gardens.

Her problems could be any or all of those.

She shook her head slowly, not wanting to dislodge his touch or break the spellbinding connection between them. "I don't know. What is it?"

"Your problem is that you've never asked enough of the people who should care for you most," he said with great feeling. "You've settled for far less than what you deserve. You allowed a man to ruin your reputation and still consider him your friend. You hold your head high when all London gossips about you behind your back. You don't blame your family for failing you when they should have rallied around you. Your betrothed betrayed and abandoned you over spurious rumors, and still, you look at me with such open, earnest trust. And you've let me kiss you and touch you when you should have slapped me for my temerity long before now.

"Your problem," he concluded, "is that you don't know your worth, when what you truly are is priceless."

He said it with such stirring, impassioned resolve, that for the span of a few rapid heartbeats, Charity could do nothing more than stare at him. Shocked and yet also moved by his insight. By the way he saw her. No one had ever called her priceless before. No one had ever thought of her worth in such a fashion.

She didn't know what to say.

So she pressed a hand over his, holding it to her cheek, relishing this closeness, the connection, the depth of emotion, until she could finally force her tongue and her mind to function again. "When this house party is over, I'm leaving for the Continent with Auntie Louise. We're planning a grand tour of our own. I don't know when, or if, I'll return to England. But what I do know, before I go, is that I want you. Just for tonight."

He sucked in a breath, almost as if she'd hit him, as if the force of her words and the revelation of her desires was like a physical blow. "You don't know what you're asking of me."

"Yes, Neville. I do. I want this. I want it with you."

His eyes closed for the second time since their conversation had begun, the golden lashes—far too long and luxurious to belong to a man—fanning over his cheeks. And when they lifted, what she saw in his unusual eyes made her heart soar. Her handsome, stern Adonis was looking at her exactly as Madeline had claimed he did earlier, just before Charity had tripped on her own hem and fallen.

In the next instant, his mouth crashed into hers, and she had her answer.

~

HIS CONTROL HAD BEEN DECIMATED.

Neville knew he shouldn't be kissing Charity now. He shouldn't allow her to remain in his room, shouldn't surrender to his own desires, and most especially not to what she'd just told him she wanted—one night with him. It was impossible, it was dangerous, it was wrong, it was a hundred kinds of foolishness, the sort that made the Venus painting scandal pale in comparison.

But he wanted her more than he'd ever believed it possible to long for another, with a potent urgency that was about so much more than the mere physical act of sexual congress. It wasn't about finding pleasure with a woman. It was about making love to Charity, and that knowledge was what ultimately proved his undoing.

He kissed her with everything he had, showing her what he felt for her. It was larger than he was, more than he could comprehend. It was elemental and divine all at once. He kissed her until he could scarcely think, and then he rose, scooping her from the chair with ease, ever cognizant of her injury.

She went willingly, no hint of protest, and he carried her to the bed, depositing her on the mattress with the greatest of care.

"You can go," he told her. "I'll carry you back to your chamber."

Her answer was to reach for the buttons on her bodice, pulling them open to reveal her lack of undergarments underneath. No corset. Not even a chemise. Her creamy breasts spilled forth, a bountiful gift he couldn't look away from or refuse. Watching her progress, he found the knot of his necktie, tugging with such vicious savagery that he hurt his neck in the process, but he didn't give a damn, pulling it free and tossing it away. He shrugged out of his coat next.

She slipped off her bodice, bare from the waist up, her skirts a cloud of silk pooling around her, no cumbersome bustle beneath. Nothing more, he'd wager, than a petticoat for shaping.

"You're beautiful," he rasped, reaching for her, his hands trembling as he cupped her breasts, running his thumbs over her pebbled nipples.

She issued a soft sound of satisfaction, her fingers making short work of the tapes on her skirts. But when she moved to rise to aid in the removal, he stayed her, splaying his hand to the smooth valley between her breasts and gently guiding her backward on the mattress until she lay flat. He swept caresses down her sides, admiring her shape and the silky softness of her bare skin.

Slowly, Neville worked her skirt and petticoat down, until she was entirely naked, and then he tenderly swung her legs onto the bed as well, taking care with her ankle. Her hair was still confined in a neat plait, curls fringing her forehead and face as she watched him from the bed. He tore at his waistcoat and shirt, throwing them to the floor without concern for the buttons he ripped away in the process.

He wanted her so much he could taste it, his heart pounding furiously in his chest, his cock painfully rigid and erect in his trousers. He had a moment of lucidity and honor, wherein he reminded himself that he hadn't gone too far yet. That he could put a stop to this madness and help her to dress.

But the sight of her, all creamy and pink loveliness on his bed, was too much for him to endure. He couldn't turn her away, couldn't end what was happening between them any more than he could derail a locomotive with his bare hands.

"Your hair," he managed somehow. "Take it down."

Slowly, with the air of a practiced seductress, she rose on bent elbows, until she rested on her forearms. With one hand, she plucked pins free, tossing them over her shoulder one at a time until they formed a rhythmic rain on the Axminster. *Plink, plink, plink.* Glorious, burnished waves fell around her shoulders and down her back. The last pin was still in midair when he shucked his trousers and joined her on the bed as naked as she was. She spread her legs as he knelt over her, and he found his place between them, a glimpse of pink, glistening folds and a pouting, plump bud filling his head with fire.

He couldn't wait another moment. He had to taste her.

Overcome by the need, he settled lower, his cock burrowing into the counterpane they hadn't bothered to turn

137

back in their eagerness. His hands were on her legs, skimming from knee to hip, then to her inner thighs, caressing, urging her to open for him completely. She did what he wanted, widening, showing herself to him without shame.

And sweet heavens above, he was lost.

Neville lowered his head and worshiped her with his tongue. One long, slow lick up her seam, the taste of her, musky and feminine and sweetly fragrant, making his cock harder still. And she was wet. Dripping. Ready for him. First, he wanted to spoil her. Wanted to show this beautiful, passionate woman just what she deserved. Not to be scorned or whispered about, but to be revered. To be adored.

To be...

Loved.

He stilled for a moment, overwhelmed by her slick heat, the taste of her on his tongue, the breathy sounds of excitement she made, the rolling of her hips. But most of all by the realization he'd just made. An odd, damning realization.

He might have somehow, entirely against his will and despite ration and reason, begun to fall in love with Lady Charity Manners. Who was he fooling? He hadn't begun to fall in love with her; he already had, fully and utterly. She was the wrong woman for him to harbor a *tendre* for; that much was certain. But it didn't matter when her fingers sifted through his hair and she shifted restlessly under him, her body seeking more.

He listened, because if there was anything Neville did well, it was that. Listened to her body's demands, to the sheer erotic joy of pleasing her. His tongue traced over the swollen bud of her sex, and then he took that sensitive bundle in his mouth and sucked. Sucked and nibbled as she came apart so sweetly for him, hips undulating to the rhythm of his tongue, her gasps falling from her lips, her fingers grasping his hair and tugging him closer until she was all there was. He was surrounded by her soft, feminine heat, by her lush legs and slick desire, by her body's ceaseless demands.

He wanted her to use him. To find her pleasure. To come, and then come again, crying out and writhing, losing herself with nothing more than his tongue to push her over the edge to her peak. When he sensed she was there, he listened to what pleased her most, applying more pressure, finding the secret place on her pearl that made her hips buck and her breath catch, made her stiffen beneath him. And then he used his teeth, alternating between licking, sucking, and biting until she cried out his name, her body quaking under his as the force of her orgasm rolled over her like a storm.

He was there for it, there for her.

Neville raised his head, drunk on Charity, his lips coated in her dew, transfixed by the erotic sight of her, naked atop his covers, legs spread wide, her breasts full and tipped with taut peaks, her hair golden on his pillow, her full, pink lips parted in wonder. He kissed her sex, suckled her bud again, and had never felt more pleased with himself. Of all the men this vibrant beauty could have had with nothing more than a quirk of her finger, she had chosen him. And he was the reason for the expression on her face, for the dark swirl of passion in her eyes, for her ragged breathing.

He thought that he could drink from her sex forever, make love to her with nothing more than his mouth, and still be fulfilled. That he could lick her until she screamed his name and the whole wing of guests came racing from their rooms, certain something was wrong. He wanted her loud and lusty, unashamed as she deserved to be. But he couldn't have her that way now. So he would settle for bringing her to her pinnacle again.

"I read about this," she murmured, still out of breath, surprising him.

But then, why should he be shocked that her curiosity

had led to her finding some ribald prose that detailed sexual congress in vivid detail? She was unabashed about her daring ways. And he admired her for it, even if he knew he ought to be properly horrified.

"What did you read about?" he asked, kissing her sex lightly, caressing her everywhere he could.

He could live here, between her legs. Never leave. He'd found paradise, and it wasn't his country estate after all. It was at the juncture of Lady Charity Manners's thighs. Venus was no competition for her.

"A man kissing a woman this way," she murmured, reaching down to tap the top of her mound with one forefinger. "Here."

The sight of her touching herself was unbearably sensual. His cock was weeping, and he had to grind it into the counterpane to stave off his own roaring need. This wasn't about him. It was about her. But no, that wasn't quite right. Rather, it was about the both of them.

He caught her finger in his mouth and sucked the tip as he'd done to her clitoris, then dragged his teeth along the fleshy pad before releasing it. "Touch yourself again. Show me."

It was a bold request. A shameful one. But Charity didn't even hesitate in giving him what he wanted, her finger settling on her mound at first. Then lower, to where her pearl protruded from the hood. She ran her finger over herself there.

He muttered something unintelligible, even to himself. A curse, a plea, he didn't know.

"Beautiful," he praised, even though he had before. He couldn't tell her enough. Admiration was a gift meant to be shared.

Neville kissed each of her inner thighs, and then, as she continued to lightly toy with herself, he kissed her opening, his tongue dipping inside to claim her the way his cock wanted to so desperately. And sweet God above, heaven and hell, it was torture and paradise, the slick warmth of her cunny, the tight heat of her passage, the way she angled her hips to bring him deeper, her inner muscles clenching on his tongue. He pointed it and fucked her that way, thrusting in and out, in and out while she strummed over her bud, her breath growing ragged again, her hips circling.

Her body was like a primed pump. This time, her release hit her swiftly. She cried out, body bowing from the bed, quivering as she rode out her spend, thrusting herself into his face so that every spare inch of him was covered in her. And then his own need roared through him, his ballocks tightening with the reminder of how very desperate his cock was to be inside her, planted deep. To claim her.

To make her his.

It was wrong, but he couldn't stop.

Neville dragged his mouth over her hip bone and kissed his way along her gorgeous body, savoring every curve, leaving the glistening evidence of her desire in his wake. He sucked her nipples and then covered her, settling between her legs, until they were hip to hip and breast to chest, his face hovering over hers as his cock pressed into her folds.

"Charity, sweetheart, are you sure?" he forced himself to ask, even though he didn't want to, part of him terrified she'd change her mind and leave him in agony.

But deep inside him, there dwelled a hint of the gentleman he'd always believed himself to be. He wouldn't take advantage. They weren't wed. Weren't even promised to each other. She'd said she only wanted one night from him, that she intended to go on a grand tour as if she were some sort of bachelor youth, sent off to explore.

He would worry about that later, when his mind was capable of functioning and forming coherent thought. For

141

now, all he could do was feel. Feel her, warm and welcoming beneath him. Hear her low, throaty voice tell him the one word he wanted most from her crushed-berry lips.

"Yes." She kissed his jaw, clutching at him wildly, as if she feared he would leave.

She needn't have labored under any such misapprehension. Not even the devil himself could pry Neville away from his present position.

He kissed her ear, reaching between their straining bodies to grasp his erect cock and run the tip through her folds, the sound of her wetness making them both groan. She felt like liquid silk. Like hot velvet. Like a dream.

"Last chance," he warned her, lips grazing the shell of her ear as he inhaled deeply, tucking the sweet rose-and-bergamot scent of her glorious hair into his lungs.

She was restless under him, wriggling, her hard nipples abrading his chest. Her hands settled on his shoulders, and then she was raking her nails down his back as if she had done so a hundred times before, spurring him on in wanton surrender.

"I won't change my mind," she told him, breathless. "I want you inside me, Neville. Now."

He was hers to command. Hers for tonight. Hers forever.

Neville positioned himself at her entrance. Her hands found his arse, and she was impatient, grasping, urging him on. He gave her what she wanted, what they both wanted, thrusting his hips and sinking into her. Shallowly at first. She stiffened, her cunny clamping around him and nearly forcing him from her body. It occurred to him then that his wild hellion was a virgin. That she was not just giving herself to him; she was giving her first time making love altogether to him.

He kissed her shoulder, her throat. "Breathe, Charity. Let me in."

She exhaled, and he inched forward, lifting his head to find her lips with his. He kissed her slowly, deeply, tenderly, showing her without words what he wanted from her, what he could give her. The pleasure of being inside her was excruciatingly good. He had to pace himself, to remember to take his time with her instead of ramming deep and losing himself the way his body screamed for him to do.

Their breaths mingled. Their tongues slid sinuously. She relaxed, the tension seeping from her. He guided her legs farther apart, then higher, around his hips. They fit together naturally. Perfectly. Another shallow thrust, and he was almost entirely seated. He wanted this to be good for her—nay, better than good. He wanted it to be wonderful.

Neville paused, tearing his mouth from hers, bussing a kiss on her cheek, her jaw. He found the hollow behind her ear, teasing it with his tongue as he slipped his fingers between them to stroke her body into the heights of pleasure again. She was still soaked, and his fingertips reveled in that wetness, playing over her demanding bud with sure motions that had her gasping and tipping up her hips to invite him the rest of the way in. The tension in her eased, and he slid deep, stretching her, filling her, her hot cunny clenched around him tightly.

He had to hold himself still for a moment, to gather his wits. Being buried in her softness, as close to her as he could be, his throbbing cock planted deep, was enough to make him lose control. And he couldn't do that.

"How are you?" he asked her, still toying with her pearl, feeling her cunny ripple and grip his length.

"I need...oh sweet heavens..."

Her response was incoherent, her breathing gratifyingly ragged.

This was good. He was bringing her pleasure instead of pain. Reassured, he moved, his cock gliding through her slick heat, finding a steady rhythm that had her gasping, her hands flying to his shoulders, her nails digging into his skin. He hoped she would mark him. He wanted to wear her passion like a tattoo—an indelible memory of the wonders of this night and this woman.

He dragged his lips back to hers, kissing her as he moved in and out, the sounds of her wetness and her breathy sighs of pleasure bringing him perilously close to the edge already. His fingers flew over her, coaxing, demanding. She stiffened under him as another orgasm seized her, and the way she tightened on his cock had him groaning into her mouth.

It was too much.

It wasn't enough.

The thin thread of his restraint snapped, and then Neville was riding her, surging into her again and again. She moved with him, her hips chasing his, back arching, her moans spurring him on. He lost himself to the intense bliss of her wrapped snugly around his cock, their bodies pumping together in tandem. Faster, deeper, harder. He forgot how to be gentle. Forgot everything but finding that mindless place where he lost himself inside her. It was here, it was now, he was going to spend. But he couldn't. Not inside her.

Frantically, he withdrew, gripping his cock, his release almost violent in its potency, his seed splashing all over her belly as he emptied himself. He dropped his face into the soft warmth of her throat, too far gone to kiss her properly, struggling to catch his breath. She wrapped her arms around him, holding him to her when he would have rolled to his side, fearful of crushing her under his weight. He stayed where she wanted him instead, absorbing the rapid beating of her heart, the rise and fall of her chest, gratitude falling over him along with the sweet languor of quenched desire.

CHAPTER 10

*C*harity woke to the faint lights of dawn brightening
the night sky around the curtains, like a watercolor
portrait encroaching on the edges of darkness. She blinked,
lucidity returning to her slowly, for she felt as if she'd slept
for days.

There was a big, warm body protectively curled around
her, and she was naked. She was sore in strange new places.

It took her a moment to realize where she was—in
Neville's bedchamber.

And that swiftly, everything that had happened the night
before returned to her in one wicked rush. The kisses, the
touches, Neville's mouth on her, kissing and licking her
everywhere. His manhood, so long and thick and beautiful,
pressing inside her, stretching her, taking her.

An answering throb came to life between her legs. His
forearm was slung around her waist possessively. She took a
moment to admire it, the golden hairs on his skin, which had
been bronzed by the sun. Last night, she'd been too overwhelmed to properly admire him. But now she turned her
head on the pillow so that she faced him, discovering that the

sun-kissed glow extended to his chest and shoulders, bared above the counterpane. He must have labored in the sun without a shirt to have achieved such color. It was wholly at odds with the tense, proper viscount she'd thought him to be.

But then, so, too, was the generous, sinful lover of the night before. There had been nothing respectable about what he had done to her, and she had loved every second. She allowed her eyes to trail over his face now in the dim morning light, noting the way slumber brought a softness to his features that was ordinarily absent. It was as if she were privy to a side of him that no one else could see, and her heart gave a pang as she thought of the other lovers who would lie here like this with him. Who would kiss him and hold him. The other lovers he would bring to the dizzying heights of orgasm, whose bodies he would worship.

The fire inside her died. She shivered, feeling suddenly far colder than the morning's chill warranted. Because she didn't want to think of him with anyone else, even if her rational mind recognized it for the reality that it was. Neville couldn't marry a scandalous woman like her, and she had no wish to wed. Adventure awaited her on the Continent, a lifetime of freedom hers to claim.

Why did the thought leave her feeling strangely unenthused?

Neville shifted, stretching, and she seized the opportunity to distract herself by admiring the flex of the muscles in his arms and chest. He made a soft sound deep in his throat, not quite a growl, and she felt an answering pulse in her core, along with the wanton urge to roll into his big body and rub herself against him.

She wanted to kiss him. To touch him.

She never wanted to leave his bed or this room.

But that was a foolish desire, and one couldn't afford to entertain because it was almost dawn, which meant the servants would soon be traversing the halls. And which greatly heightened the risk of her being seen leaving his chamber and returning to her own. That was a scandal she wouldn't risk—for Neville's sake and for Margaret's, too.

He opened his eyes, the light green searing her to her soul in a new way this morning as they met hers. "Morning."

His voice was gruff and low from sleep, and she felt it like a caress.

"Good morning." Her hand settled over his arm, still wrapped snugly around her waist, keeping her there. "I should go."

Her heart felt heavy at the thought, a leaden weight dragging her down.

He kissed her shoulder, silent for a moment, before a heavy sigh left him. "Ah God. What have I done?"

When he began to slide his arm away, she held it there, not ready for him to release her just yet. "You did what I wanted you to do. What *we* wanted to do." She smiled teasingly. "What you wanted to do since you saw me swimming that morning."

He regarded her solemnly, his expression inscrutable. "What I wanted to do since I first saw you when we arrived."

His words gave her pause; he hadn't paid her much notice when he had come to Sherborne Manor with Margaret. She'd been teasing Lady Edith about her reading proclivities in the great hall—likely too loudly, as she did most things—when he had swept over the threshold, alarmingly handsome, all rigid hauteur.

"I didn't think you noticed me that day."

Neville gave her a crooked smile that was almost boyish, so much more at ease than he ordinarily was, his dimples making a rare appearance. "Sweetheart, it's impossible *not* to notice you."

She found herself smiling back at him, warmed by his words. "Because I'm wretchedly ill-mannered, likely."

At least, according to most of her family.

"No, because you're bold and daring and beautiful and kind." He was serious, holding her gaze so there could be no doubt of the validity of his words or his own belief in them. "You're everything a lady should be, and you're unapologetically you. I admire you for that. You're far braver than I've ever been."

But that wasn't true. He *was* brave. They both carried scars on their hearts from their pasts. And she admired him for the man he was.

"Thank you," she told him simply, held captive by his stare.

The air between them changed. The drowsy ease of slumber had fled him. He was awake, his eyes sharp and clear. And his body was radiating heat that she wanted to burn her.

"You needn't thank me, Charity. It's the truth." The other side of his mouth kicked up in a self-deprecating grin. "Flattery is beyond me, I'm afraid. I've never been a silver-tongued charmer."

Her hand drifted down his arm, past his wrist, until she could twine her fingers through his. Their palms met, perfectly aligned, his hand dwarfing hers. Capable of so much strength, so much gentleness. Capable of bringing her such great pleasure.

"I like you just as you are," she told him, the closest she dared come to making a true admission of just how deeply her feelings for him ran, like the roots of a tree, spreading and reaching into the furthest, darkest depths of her being.

They stared at each other, the silence thick and rife with meaning. She was busy committing his face to memory, the way he looked, golden hair ruffled and falling rakishly over his brow, his eyes dark with desire, the prickle of stubble on his sharp jaw. He felt like he was hers this morning, and she felt like she was his.

Without saying a word, he used their linked hands to roll her toward him. She went from her back to her side, and he met her halfway, their noses so close they almost brushed, their mouths a scant inch apart.

He kissed her then, and all the desire from the night before returned a hundredfold because now her body had been awakened to passion. She was intensely aware of every part of her that longed for his touch, from her breasts to her nipples, to the apex of her thighs, where she was already wet and aching.

His tongue was in her mouth, his hand cupping her nape. Leaving was suddenly the last thing on her mind. All she wanted to do was linger with him, to kiss him and make love with him again.

He ended the kiss before she was ready, nuzzling her cheek, the rasp of his whiskers on her skin a divine torture. "Don't go yet."

"I won't." The words left her before she could think better of them. Before she could think at all.

Neville kissed the corner of her lips, her jaw, her throat, his breath falling hot on her skin. "Don't go ever."

"I wish I didn't have to."

But there were realities awaiting them. Realities that could wait a few minutes longer. She prayed for the sun to slow its ascent, for the servants to oversleep, for time to halt.

He released her hand then, gliding it beneath the counterpane and smooth, soft sheets to touch her. The graze of his fingers over her breast made her gasp with pleasure, and when he took her nipple between his thumb and forefinger, plucking and rolling the sensitive peak, her gasp turned into a throaty moan. His caress glided over the dip of her waist, along her hip, and then across her belly before dipping between her legs. He parted her folds, sending a jolt of need through her, unerringly finding the bud of her sex.

She arched into his touch and, growing bolder, allowed her own hand to slide under the covers. She found the muscled wall of his chest, the crisp hair tickling her palm. He was so hot, his body hard and masculine and yet sleek. She followed the plane of his abdomen lower, and then his cock was there, erect and smooth and unlike anything she'd ever touched. She wrapped her hand around him as she'd watched him do to himself the night before when they had made love, gratified by the growl rumbling from his chest.

"I love the way you feel," she whispered, stroking him from root to tip, wishing they were free of the counterpane so that she could see him as she touched him, but settling for what she could have with their time rapidly dwindling.

Her words seemed to have an effect on him, for his cock grew in her hand, thickening and elongating. There was so much of him. It was almost impossible to believe he had fit inside her. Little wonder she was sore and aching in places she'd never been before. Neville was a large man everywhere.

He made a sound of appreciation, his fingers moving over her with expert ease. "Tell me what you want, Charity."

"More," she whispered. "One more time before I go."

Yes, that was what she longed for more than anything. Surely they had time.

He rolled to his back, his hand leaving her sex. But before she could protest, he caught her waist in a firm but gentle grip, moving her so that she was atop him, the coverlets pooling around both their waists. Her legs moved to either side of his, her hand still on him, stroking.

"Take what you want," he said, lying there in rakish splendor, naked and so handsome, her proper, rule-following Adonis who had thrown caution to the wind for her.

"I don't know how," she admitted. "I read about it being done this way, but how will you fit?"

"Of course you did." He grinned at her, caressing her hips, her waist, cupping her breasts and rolling his thumbs over her nipples. "Where the devil have you been finding all these wicked books?"

"I borrow them from my aunt's collection. She doesn't know, of course."

Not that Auntie Louise would frown on her efforts to educate herself on such matters. But Charity knew her parents would have been furious with her aunt, had they discovered she'd provided Charity with forbidden literature. So Charity simply hadn't asked, sparing Auntie Louise the embarrassment.

"I shouldn't be surprised," Neville said, his voice thick with desire. "Do you want to try it like this, with you astride me? You'll be the one in control of the pace, of your pleasure."

Her inner muscles clenched at his words. She liked the idea very much.

"Yes. Please."

He flipped the coverlets back, the cool air kissing her skin as she was suddenly entirely bared to him, every part of her on display. How beautiful he was, big and strong, lying on his back, his gaze burning into hers, his hands coasting over her, making her desperate for more.

"Rise on your knees," he directed.

She did as he asked, her hand still on his cock, stroking. There was a bead of moisture at the tip that fascinated her. She wanted to taste it, to lick him there. To pleasure him as he had her. She knew, too, that it was an act that gave a man great pleasure. But their current positions didn't allow her the freedom to try. Later, she thought, and then instantly realized that there could be no

SCARLETT SCOTT

other such idyll for them. That this was all they were meant to have.

The reminder sent a sharp pang of sadness through her.

But then he pinched her nipples lightly, and the sadness dissipated in favor of the lust that was roaring through her.

"Put my cock inside you."

His low, wicked instruction made her cunny tighten and pulse with need. She wanted him in her again, wanted to take her pleasure.

One more time, she told herself. Then never again. She had to make the most of it. To seize what remained of the night before the sun stole it from her.

She guided his cock to her entrance, the thick tip of him glancing over her sensitive skin. Instinct took over. Panting with need, she pressed his erection into her, until part of him was lodged inside her, her cunny stretching to accommodate him as it had the night before.

"Now, lower yourself all the way," he urged, flexing his hands on her hips, showing her how to move.

She sank down, and he was inside her, fully sheathed. She was full of him, impaled on his cock, and he was reaching a new part of her that was exquisitely sensitive. He was leading her on, telling her what to do, and yet she was the one who was commanding their mutual pleasure. She was the one in control.

"I'm yours," he murmured, as if sensing the tenor of her thoughts. "Do what you will with me."

He didn't need to say more, and Charity had no way to answer him, save one—with movement, with her body taking his, claiming it as surely as he had hers. She rocked on him, the pressure so intense that it thieved her breath and her wits. Until she was drunk on pleasure, on him. On her sweet viscount who was all wrong for her and yet oh-so-very right.

She rode him, his hands helping her to find a pace. Up, then down. His cock sliding with impossible precision as she rose, then sank down upon him again. Each thrust brought her closer to the edge, her belly tightening, her sex pulsing, her release almost upon her. He pulled her toward him, catching one of her nipples in his mouth and sucking hard, his hands coasting over the small of her back and up and down her spine, allowing her free rein as she found her rhythm. She'd never felt more powerful, as if she'd been made for this man, their bodies fitting together in perfect rightness.

She was close, so close. He sensed her need, one of his hands coming between them, his fingers flying over her pearl until the pleasure coiling inside her could no longer be contained. With a cry, she found her release, rocking on him, her heart thundering with the force of it, bliss bursting over her like fireworks in a night sky. She collapsed against him, breathing as ragged as if she'd just swum the length of the Sherborne Manor lake twice over. And he held her to him, kissing her softly, sweetly, before rolling them as one so that she was on her back now, his hard, thick shaft still lodged deep inside her.

Belatedly, she realized he hadn't found his own release yet. But Neville was considerate and gentlemanly even in his lovemaking. He didn't take without giving, and he always put her needs first. How grateful she was for him, for these stolen moments, for the chance to know him so intimately and be so transformed. To be held by him, kissed by him, loved by him.

Her heart gave a pang that he banished with kisses. Hot, hard, and demanding kisses that stole her breath all over again as his fingers returned to her bud, resuming their relentless teasing. The rasp of his callused thumb over her made her gasp. The way he thrust deeper inside her made her moan.

She held to him tightly, her lips seeking his, and the pleasure somehow, impossibly, began to build anew until she thought she might explode with it. Or catch fire. Dimly, through the haze of her pleasure-drunk mind, she was aware that she needed to savor their lovemaking, to commit every breath, each touch, the heady sensation of him moving within her to memory so that she would never forget.

He gave her his tongue, and she sucked on it, her hands on his shoulders, then down his back. She dragged her nails over his skin, and he groaned, low and feral, his thrusts harder and faster. Noises fled her. His thumb worked her pearl. And then, suddenly, it was upon her again.

She came on a cry that was far too loud, and he swallowed it with his kisses, his body above her, over her, in her. Claiming her in a way no one ever had and no one else ever would. It was too much. She thought she might die from it. But oh, what a death it would be.

Neville withdrew suddenly, and she knew the hot spurt of his release painting her folds and inner thigh, sending a new series of quivers through her. He rolled off her, his chest rising and falling as harshly as hers, landing on his back at her side. And she lay there for a few, purloined moments, the sun rising ever higher beyond the curtains, steadily banishing a night she never wanted to end.

It was then that she made a stunning realization.

She was in love with Neville.

~

CHARITY LIMPED into her bedroom with nary a minute to spare, whirling over the threshold and snapping the door closed at her back as she rested against it, breathing a sigh of relief. No one had spied her on the perilous journey back to her own chamber. Not even a servant had been about. Her secret was safe. Not a soul knew she'd spent the night in Neville's bed, in his arms.

And part of the morning, too.

"Where have you been?"

The firm, disapproving voice made her jump and gasp, her hand pressed to her galloping heart. She wasn't alone. Someone else was in her bedroom, seated in one of the wing-back chairs by the hearth, illuminated by a thin slat of early-morning light slipping through a gap in the curtains.

Someone all too familiar.

"Auntie Louise," she said weakly. "What are you doing here?"

Her aunt rose from the chair, her countenance as grim as Charity had ever seen it. "Waiting for you, my dear. You didn't answer my question. Where have you been?"

The truth was out of the question, even if lying to her aunt filled her with a mixture of guilt and dread.

"I went for a walk," she blurted, using the first excuse that emerged in her befuddled mind.

"You're lying to me."

Of course she was.

"I couldn't sleep," she continued, forcing a smile. "The dawn air is so restorative, I find."

"The hall air, or the air in the bedchamber of a certain gentleman?" Auntie Louise asked, crossing the room in measured strides.

Charity's stomach clenched. "Auntie Louise, why would you suggest—"

"Because I'm not a fool, Charity," her aunt interrupted sharply, though she took care to keep her voice from carrying. "And because I was young and careless once, too. I know what it feels like, what it looks like. I know when you're

155

telling a lie and when you've been sneaking away with a gentleman."

Oh dear.

She swallowed hard. "I was hardly sneaking away with anyone."

Auntie Louise stopped before her, tilting her head and pinning Charity with a knowing stare that was far too much like her own. "Shall we talk about what else I know?"

The door at her back felt like a trap, all the wonder of the morning effectively expelled. "Auntie, I can't begin to imagine what you're speaking of."

"Your behavior is what I'm speaking of," her aunt elaborated, unsmiling. "Morning swims in the lake in your chemise, disappearing into the maze with Lord Wilton—"

"I didn't disappear into the maze with him," she interrupted, aghast at the thought that her aunt might have been watching her far more closely than she'd realized and that she might truly have more than just a suspicion of what Charity had been doing and where she'd been.

"I watched you from an upstairs window."

"Oh." She bit her lip, for there was no arguing what Auntie Louise had seen with her own eyes.

"Yes, *oh*." Auntie Louise planted her hands on her waist. "And your hair was terribly mussed when you emerged sometime later. It was plain to see what you'd been doing in that maze with him. As for the swimming, I can only hope you had no witnesses. Yes, my dear. I've been watching you because it's my duty to see that nothing ill befalls you. I didn't object to the swimming or the disappearing, nor even to kisses with the viscount, because I thought it was innocent fun. I believed him to be a gentleman of morals, a man who takes propriety seriously."

"He is," she protested. "He's proper and staid."

Well, not entirely proper and staid. With sufficient impetus, Neville was quite deliciously wicked. And she liked that hidden facet of him.

"Not if he allowed you to visit him in his bedchamber last night," Auntie Louise countered quietly. "Not if you spent the night there with him."

Oh good heavens. It was worse than she'd thought. Charity had to look away from her aunt's disappointed gaze, directing her stare to the floor instead. And that was when she realized the buttons on her bodice were misaligned. Off by two. In her haste to dress in the shadows of Neville's chamber after they had made love for the second time, she had failed to button herself properly. And she hadn't even noticed.

"Lord Wilton did nothing of the sort," she squeaked out.

Hopefully Auntie Louise wouldn't spy the error. Charity swept past her aunt, moving to the window, hastily trying to rectify the matter while her back was to Auntie Louise. She feigned interest in the window dressings, fingers flying over fastenings.

"You needn't bother with the buttons," Auntie Louise said from behind, her tone somber. "I know it wasn't the handiwork of your lady's maid."

"Blast," she muttered, giving up and thrusting open the curtains instead.

The sun was far too bright, shining directly into her eyes and making her squint. Where was the rain and dreariness when one needed it?

Her aunt joined her at the window, casting a knowing look in her direction. "What am I to tell your mother and father, dear heart?"

"Nothing," she said hastily. "You needn't say a word of what has happened here to them. They don't care about me anyway. They're far too busy with everyone else to notice me."

Her aunt's lips tightened into a stern line. "Charity, when you lie with a man, you can become with child. You are aware of that, are you not? Unlike most of your scrapes, this is the sort that can have lifelong implications and consequences."

Her cheeks went hot. "Not if he doesn't...if he finishes...elsewhere."

Words she'd hoped never to have to speak to her aunt. But she knew that from her books as well. Auntie Louise's books, as it happened.

Her aunt paled. "I don't wish to know how you garnered that understanding of matters."

"From your books," she blurted.

Auntie Louise stared at her, mouth agape. "Charity!"

"It was a mistake, the first one I took," she explained. "I was bored and looking for something to read that wasn't tedious. You'd left it in the blue salon. After that, I noticed the bookshelves in your bedchamber and realized there were more of them." Guilt assailed her, making her reveal all. "I became astonishingly adept at removing one and replacing it with another after I'd finished with it. I didn't think you'd ever noticed, and I knew that if you had, you would have likely blamed it on my brother or one of the footmen."

"For how long?" her aunt demanded curtly.

"Since I was fifteen," she admitted.

"My God, I've failed you. You were doomed to repeat my sins from the start."

"Your sins?" Charity frowned, struggling to understand. "Whatever do you mean?"

Her auntie Louise had never married; she'd lived with Charity for as long as she could recall, a maiden aunt fixture of the household. And whilst she was always garrulous and wore bold colors and never shied from fun, often entertaining Charity and her older siblings in a way their parents would never lower themselves to do, she was hardly a sinner.

"Nothing." Auntie Louise shook her head, blinking furiously. "You must forget I ever said it."

And that was when Charity realized her aunt had tears welling in her eyes. Why? Because she had stolen some of Auntie Louise's vulgar books? Because Charity had disappointed her? Because she'd spent the night with a man out of wedlock?

"I've upset you." Charity reached for her aunt, placing a comforting hand on her arm. "Forgive me, Auntie. I never should have taken the books without your approval."

"It's not the books I'm concerned about, Charity. It's that you spent all of last night in Lord Wilton's bedroom with him. Alone."

"Nothing untoward occurred," she tried weakly.

Auntie Louise covered Charity's hand with her own, holding her stare. "Don't lie to me. I need to know the extent of the damage done."

"There's no chance I can be with child," she reassured her aunt.

"That's not what I'm asking, and you know it."

Oh dear heavens. Auntie Louise was going to make her say it. Heat crept up her throat, over her face. Even her ears seemed to be ablaze as thoughts of what had happened between herself and Neville burned her mind, making her hot all over.

"Auntie," she protested.

"Did you give yourself to the viscount? And don't lie to me, Charity Prudence Manners. I can tell when you're deceiving me. You bite your lower lip and look to the left."

"I don't do that," she denied, then realized she had been chewing on her lip, her gaze straying to the left side of the chamber.

Drat her aunt, forever too clever.

"Charity." Auntie Louise cocked her head, her expression stern. "Tell me the truth."

"Yes," she admitted at last. "But you needn't worry. It won't happen again."

"Not without the benefit of marriage, it won't," Auntie Louise growled. "And to think that I imagined Lord Wilton was a gentleman of principle. How dare he dishonor you so thoroughly—and at a house party, no less—whilst his own niece is in residence? I'll find him and box his ears."

Auntie Louise was in a fine rage, turning away from Charity in a sweep of black skirts that matched her current funereal mood. But when she stalked across the Axminster, intent, apparently, upon finding Neville and giving him a dressing down, Charity rushed after her, wincing at the pain in her ankle even as she stayed her aunt's progress.

"Wait, Auntie Louise. You can't go rushing off to him and box his ears. It wasn't Neville's idea. It was mine. I'm the one who went to his bedchamber last night. I took him by surprise."

"You know how wretchedly you've been treated over that dreadful painting. What will it be like if you're carrying his child out of wedlock? Do you think he will come rushing to your side and marry you? Do you think you'll be able to keep your baby as an unmarried mother, alone in the world, without everyone spurning both you and the innocent child?"

Auntie Louise's voice trembled from the force of her emotion, and the tears had returned, not just glittering in her blue eyes now, but slipping down her cheeks. Charity had never seen her in such a state.

The truth was, she hadn't thought about a child. Hadn't thought about consequences. She'd only thought about what she wanted. And that had been Neville.

"Auntie, please. You're overset," she said calmly, blinking at the sting in her own eyes. "Have a seat, and I'll ring for tea to calm you. The servants should be about by now."

"I don't want tea, my dear girl. I want to be assured you won't fall into the same ruthless trap your mother did." Auntie Louise pressed the back of her hand over her lips suddenly after her last curious pronouncement, almost as if she wished she could recall the words.

For all their faults where she was concerned, her mother and father had a rare, loving marriage. As far as Charity knew, neither had strayed. Which meant...

Charity's brow furrowed. "My mother? What do you mean? Did Mother have a child before she married Father?"

It seemed an impossibility. And yet that was what Auntie Louise had inferred.

"You mustn't think of it," Auntie Louise said, pale again. "I misspoke."

"No," Charity said slowly, turning her aunt's words over in her mind, struggling to make sense of them. "I don't think you did. What are you saying, Auntie? That my mother had a bastard child she was forced to give away?"

"No, darling," her aunt said quietly, her face graver than Charity had ever seen it, all the good cheer and levity that were her hallmarks shockingly absent. "I'm saying that *I* had a bastard child I was forced to give away."

Charity stared at her aunt, a strange, almost sickening sensation dawning on her. A suspicion which, if it were true, meant that her entire life had been a lie. That everything she'd known had been one vast, devastating and carefully constructed falsehood.

"You had a child," she repeated hoarsely, feeling as if she were seeing Auntie Louise—truly seeing her—for the first time.

The golden hair that had a marked determination to curl.

The love of vibrant colors.

The blue eyes.

The voice that no one could tell apart from Charity's when they were in another room.

Her nose, the freckles that plagued her if she ventured into the sun without a well-brimmed hat.

Her love of naughty books and reading and water—Auntie Louise loved to fish and swim and go boating.

"I did," Auntie Louise confirmed quietly. "I do. And it has been my greatest joy to watch her grow into womanhood. But it has also been my greatest devastation to do so as someone other than her mother. I don't want that for you, Charity. It will tear you apart. Wilton has to marry you. There's no other option for the two of you now. I'll see to it."

Charity was reeling. But not because of her aunt's determination that she and Neville marry. Because she feared she understood what her aunt was truly saying, without uttering the words.

"You didn't rest until I told you the truth," she said, her voice quavering. "Now it's your turn to do the same. Your child…you said you've watched her grow as someone other than her mother. What does that mean?"

"It means she doesn't know I'm her mother," Auntie Louise said.

"Who is she?" Charity whispered, already knowing the answer.

It had been plain as day. It was staring at her now, with a face that resembled hers far more than either her mother's or her father's ever had.

"She's you, Charity," Auntie Louise admitted, a hitch in her voice. "She's you."

A rush of emotion hit her. Shock. Anger. Confusion. So much that she was shaking with it. Trembling, her mind blank as a page waiting for words to be written upon it.

"You're…my mother?"

The woman she'd known as her aunt all her life nodded. "Yes."

With a sob, Charity rushed past her, not knowing anything other than that she'd been lied to for so long. And she needed to escape. To walk. To think. She needed to be alone.

"Charity, where are you going?" Auntie Louise—her *mother*—called after her. "Wait, please. Let me explain."

But Charity didn't stop. She threw open the door and rushed from the chamber as fast as her sprained ankle would allow, down the hall to the grand staircase. She raced down the steps as quickly as she could, rushing through the great hall, all the way to the exterior door, not even caring that she didn't have shoes. Out into the rising sun she went, the start of the day she'd dreaded. She didn't stop running until she was outside, the cool morning air on her cheeks, the ground punishing and wet beneath her bare feet.

She ran and she ran and she ran, until her lungs burned from the effort and her ankle was aching and the soles of her feet were cut and bruised. And then she threw herself to the ground beneath the leafy boughs of a wizened old oak and drew her knees to her chest, hugging herself as she burst into tears.

CHAPTER 11

*N*eville woke to an empty bed that smelled of Charity's sweet floral perfume, an aching cock-stand, the morning sun burning through the curtains with all its recriminations, and a gut heavy with regret.

She was gone.

Which meant that after he'd fallen deep into a sated slumber, she'd slipped from his chamber. And on her injured ankle, which was likely still paining her. When he'd said nothing of his feelings or his intentions, which were more than clear now that he was lucid enough to think. In the absence of temptation, a man's brain worked damned well. Pity his hadn't been functioning earlier.

After they had made love for the second time before dawn, he had tended to her, and then he had tucked her into his arms. They'd lain together, both of them dreading the rising sun and the necessity that they part. And yet being wrapped in her embrace had felt so good, so right, that he had allowed himself to drift asleep.

It certainly hadn't been what he had wanted to do.

He had meant to talk to her about the future. For surely

she could not wish to go on her grand tour with her aunt after everything they had shared. She felt something for him, he knew it. And he…well, it was plain as the sun risen high in the Yorkshire sky that he had fallen ridiculously, foolishly, madly in love with her.

He wanted to make her his wife.

He wanted to spend his life with her. To wake with her in his arms, in his bed. To kiss her awake and kiss her to sleep. Wanted more than he had ever supposed himself capable of wanting.

But first, he had to find her and convince her that she wanted all those things too. That she wanted him, puns and all. He hoped he was capable of such a feat. God knew he was no matrimonial prize. Charity, with all her vibrant boldness, and himself, with his awkward lack of town bronze, his social niceties spare and almost nonexistent. He had to try, however.

And to do that, he had to dress himself and get out of this bloody bed.

He tossed back the bedclothes, performed cursory ablutions, and threw on his clothing himself, not bothering to ring for his valet or even shave. There wasn't time. He needed to find Charity forthwith.

With haste, he left his bedchamber, stalking down the hall as he consulted his pocket watch—half past nine. Despicably late. Charity would likely be in the breakfast room by now, already having had her swim in the lake. Had she swum in the lake this morning? There was a distinct chill in the air; if she had, she'd be fortunate if she didn't come down with a lung infection. She needed to take better care of herself, by God.

He didn't want her flitting about alone at dawn any longer. She was his to protect, and he intended to do so. He had no doubt she was going to put up a fight about that, but they could compromise. He would stand sentinel as she swam, make certain she was safe.

Neville was so caught up in his thoughts that he didn't notice the lone female figure tucked into a chair in an alcove until she spoke as he passed.

"Lord Wilton."

He paused and turned, the voice familiar and so like Charity's that he might have mistaken it, were he not looking at her aunt. Lady Louise Manners was as lovely as her niece, her beauty bearing the dignity of age. But it wasn't her resemblance to Charity or her loveliness that he took note of just now. Rather, it was her countenance.

She was pale, her cheeks tearstained, her eyes puffy, her gaze raw.

"My lady." He bowed, hastening to her, fear making his gut clench. He was thinking of Charity in that blasted lake. What if she'd become caught in something beneath the water? Sweet God. "What's amiss?" he asked as she rose from her seat. "Is it Lady Charity?"

"Yes," she said simply.

The old fear hit him like a blow, the memories of the day his brother had disappeared in the pond. Of the way his small body had looked, pale and waterlogged, as the gardeners pulled him from the water.

"What is it?" he demanded, fear making his voice hoarse yet harsh. "Tell me. Did she go to the lake this morning? Has something happened to her?"

He couldn't bear the notion. His mouth was dry as cotton, his hands trembling, his pocket watch still clutched cold and hard in his palm, the gold biting into his skin.

"I don't know where she is," Lady Louise said grimly, unsmiling. "Come with me, my lord. This is a discussion that necessitates privacy."

"She's not..." His words trailed off. Neville couldn't bring himself to finish the sentence, to say the words. A cold sweat had broken out on his brow, and his stomach was queasy.

"Come," Lady Louise repeated.

He tucked his pocket watch into his waistcoat belatedly and offered his arm. She accepted it, and they began moving down the hall.

"There's a sitting room at the end of the portrait gallery," she said. "We can go there to speak."

"Of course." Her stern mien wasn't doing anything to improve the irrational fears still churning within him, but he had no choice other than to accept Lady Louise's word that no harm had befallen Charity.

Still, where was she? What was going on?

They passed through the portrait gallery, the unsmiling faces of generations of Dukes and Duchesses of Bradford watching in silent, eternal condemnation. At last, they reached the sitting room Lady Louise had spoken of, finding it blessedly empty. He escorted her inside and closed the door firmly behind them before turning to Charity's aunt.

"Now then, my lady, what is the cause for your distress?"

"We should sit, Lord Wilton." Lady Louise's voice was unusually frigid as she gestured to the seating area by the hearth.

Understanding crept over him suddenly. Lady Louise's pallor, her forbidding expression, the ice in her tone. She must have been waiting for him in that alcove. Why else would she have been there? And he had been too caught up in worry for Charity to realize the gravity of the situation.

Lady Louise *knew*.

"After you, my lady," he managed, gesturing politely to the seating arrangement.

"Thank you." With stilted formality that was unusual for her, she sat in one of the wingback chairs, gripping the arms tightly with both hands.

He sat as well, near enough that she could slap him if she wished. He wouldn't blame her. He had dishonored her niece. If ever a man had deserved a slap, it was Neville. Well, Neville and that bastard Ainsley, who had thrown Charity over because of a silly rumor. What a bloody fool. He deserved a blackened eye.

He cleared his throat. "Lady Louise, let me preface this discussion by saying that I hold your niece in the highest regard. She's not just the most beautiful woman I've ever met, she's also the most vibrant and caring. She is intelligent, confident, and I admire her more than words can possibly convey. Indeed, during this house party, as impossible and hasty as it may seem, I've fallen in love with her."

Lady Louise's lower lip trembled for a moment, before she gathered her composure. "Of course you've fallen in love with her, my lord. Charity has a way with everyone, and after watching the two of you together, I can't say I'm surprised. What does surprise me, and disappoints me most severely, is the recklessness with which you've treated her."

Guilt made his gut clench. "You are correct in your censure, my lady. Please accept my heartfelt apologies, along with my promise that I will rectify my actions as soon as I'm able. And, God willing, Lady Charity agrees."

Lady Louise's blue gaze was searching. "You intend to marry her, then?"

"Nothing would bring me greater happiness than making her my wife." As he said the words, the truth of them settled into him. He felt it in his bones, the very rightness of it.

He had come to Sherborne Manor with Margaret's future in mind, above his own. He hadn't expected to find a woman who made him feel the way Charity did. And yet he had somehow discovered a part of himself he'd never known was missing until he had seen her that first day from across the great hall. His lungs had seized, his heart beating fast, and when their gazes had collided across the vast chamber, he had felt the connection between them as surely as a touch. He had dismissed the fanciful notion, of course. She had been teasing her bespectacled friend, Lady Edith, about a medical treatise, her laughter echoing off the walls and marble floor, and he'd been reluctantly entranced.

"Thank heavens," Lady Louise said, all the stiffness seeping out of her bearing, her shoulders dipping as she sighed heavily. "It's been my greatest fear, you see, Charity suffering for her rebellious nature as I did. A man can sow his seed as he wishes without a thought for the consequences. He can sire a hundred bastards, and society and fortune will still smile upon him, as if he's done nothing untoward. But for a woman, all it requires is one mistake. One passing fancy that goes too far, and she reaps the pain for a lifetime. It never leaves her. In this world of ours, a woman can never be forgiven for her sins."

There was something beneath the surface of Lady Louise's words, an edge to her tone, that told Neville she wasn't merely speaking in the abstract sense. Rather, she was speaking from experience. The pain in her eyes, in her voice, couldn't be denied.

"You needn't fear such an outcome befalling Lady Charity," he reassured her gently. "I make mistakes as easily as any man, but I do hold fast to my honor. You have my word as a gentleman that I would never hurt her."

Lady Louise nodded, then blinked furiously. He realized she was holding back tears.

Neville reached into his coat, extracting a handkerchief, and offered it to her. "For you, my lady."

She accepted it graciously, dabbing at her eyes as she struggled to maintain her composure. "Thank you, Lord Wilton. I trust you're being honest with me now and that you have every intention of coming up to scratch."

"I do," he reassured her with a vehemence that startled even himself.

She nodded. "The Earl of Ainsley broke her heart, and I could do nothing to stop it. I saw it happening before she did —he was a worthless fribble and a preening peacock who only cared about the way the rest of society looked upon him. But she was young and naïve, and he fooled her with his charm. You're nothing like him, thank heavens. You may be handsome, but you're no useless fop, and what you lack in charm, you make up for in intellect."

Neville wasn't certain if he ought to be honored or insulted by Lady Louise's assessment. He decided it didn't matter. All that *did* matter was finding Charity and convincing her to marry him, making things right between them.

"He wasn't worthy of her," he said, thoughts of Ainsley making his jaw clench.

He had never been a violent man, but he was reasonably certain he would deliver the earl the drubbing of his life, given half the chance.

"No." Lady Louise smiled sadly at him. "He wasn't." She paused, sighing heavily, looking torn. "There's something else I must tell you, Lord Wilton. A secret that you must guard with your very life. If anyone were to find out the truth of what I'm about to tell you, many lives would be ruined."

"I'll not speak a word of what is said in this room," he promised. "I vow it."

She nodded again, giving him another searching look, as if making certain he was as trustworthy as she hoped. "When I saw you and Charity yesterday, I had a suspicion something was afoot between the two of you. She thinks I'm an absent chaperone, too busy in the card room to know what she's about, but I've been watching her. I know her better than anyone. Better, even, than she knows herself. Because I was just like her once. I, too, was young and wild and wayward. I wore my heart on my sleeve and never gave a thought for the future. Last night, I couldn't shake the feeling that something was wrong. So I went to her bedchamber, just after midnight. She wasn't there."

Neville knew precisely where she had been. In his bedroom. With him.

"I stayed there all night," Lady Louise continued, "waiting for her to return. And when she finally did at dawn, I'm afraid I was beside myself with worry. I said things I shouldn't have. I revealed a secret I've been keeping for five-and-twenty years."

He tensed, gripping the arms of his chair, sudden prescience washing over him as he thought about the emotion in Lady Louise's voice, the way she had spoken of consequences for women but not for men, Charity's absence, Lady Louise's tearstained face. All the similarities between the two women.

"My God," he said hoarsely. "You're her mother, aren't you?"

"Yes." Lady Louise looked stricken as she confirmed his suspicion. "I am. I told her this morning. I didn't intend to do so. I promised my brother when he agreed to raise her as his own that I would never tell her the true circumstances of her birth. He feared it would tear her apart. Perhaps it has. She fled from her chamber, my lord. The servants told me she raced through the front door without a word to them. She wasn't even wearing any shoes."

"Her ankle."

And God, her feet.

Her *heart*.

The shock of making such a discovery. Neville couldn't begin to comprehend the effect it must have had on her.

"She'll injure it worse, I fear," Lady Louise said. "It's all my fault. I was at sixes and sevens, and I didn't take care with what I was saying. I'm afraid she'll do something reckless, but I didn't want to raise the alarm in the household. I couldn't bear to create another scandal that would hurt her worse than that blasted Venus painting did."

He rose from the chair, knowing he needed to get to Charity, posthaste. "I'll look for her, my lady. I won't stop looking until I find her."

"Thank you, Lord Wilton." Lady Louise dabbed at her cheeks and a fresh rush of tears, looking helpless and alone.

"You needn't thank me. It's the least I can do." With a bow, he took his leave and then stalked from the room, traveling as quickly as his long-legged strides would allow.

∾

At her side, Honoré the swan trumpeted, the sound carrying across the surface of the man-made lake.

"You can say that again," Charity agreed, reaching for the swan and gently petting his snowy feathers with the backs of her fingers once, then a second time more hesitantly.

She stopped when Honoré turned his attention to her, pinning her with a hesitant glare. She turned her hand palm up, allowing him to nibble at her for a moment with his beak as she'd learned he was wont to do, before she resumed her gentle strokes. He turned his head and trumpeted again, permitting the touch with obvious, regal reluctance.

Charity sniffled. The hours she'd spent weeping had rendered her nose quite disagreeably clogged. The swan's presence had been an unexpected comfort. Her eyes ached. Her head hurt. But it was her heart that was most bruised and painful.

Her life had been a lie.

Everyone close to her had deceived her. She wondered if her siblings knew they weren't siblings at all, but rather cousins. And Auntie Louise—to carry on all these years in such a pretense. How could she have done so?

Oh, she knew there would have been reasons for the duplicity. If Charity had been born a bastard for all the world to know, she would have been ostracized from society before she'd been old enough to enter it. And so, too, Auntie Louise. The secret would have been meant to protect not just Charity, but Louise as well.

Auntie Louise, her true mother.

In the wake of the massive shock that had overwhelmed her at the revelation, Charity could acknowledge that the woman she'd known as her aunt had always been the mother of her heart. They had shared a bond unlike anything Charity had known with the rest of her family. Perhaps a part of her had always known, or at least suspected, the truth, as impossible as it seemed.

But that didn't mean she was ready to forgive just yet. Nor that she could wrap her mind around the implications. In the span of one day, her life had changed irrevocably. She had realized she'd fallen in love, she had made love for the first time, and she had learned a devastating family secret.

Neville.

A morning that had begun with such promise had been thoroughly set aflame by the discovery that she wasn't who she thought she was. Heavens, she wasn't even Lady Charity Manners. Her mother had never married. She'd been born a bastard, and only Auntie Louise—her mother, she reminded herself bitterly—knew her father's surname. Now, she was left with nothing more than ashes.

Honoré trumpeted again, as if in outraged protest.

"You as well, Honoré," she told him, giving him another light caress. "Ashes and you. That's all I have remaining."

173

"And me, as well."

The deep, masculine voice behind her gave Charity a start. The swan flapped his wings in warning and hissed. She turned to see Neville standing at a discreet distance, looking unfairly handsome in his country tweed. Her heart tripped over itself at the sight of him.

"Neville," she greeted, thinking of the sight she must present, hair unbound, hanging down her back in wild tangles from the night before, her bodice misbuttoned, her eyes swollen and red from weeping. "What are you doing here?"

"Looking for you," he said simply, striding forward until Honoré gave another vexed flap, puffing himself up as if he fully intended to attack a man who was many times his size and far stronger.

If she hadn't been mired in so much misery, Charity might have laughed at the prospect of man versus swan.

"Why?" she asked, sniffling again and dabbing at her cheeks with the back of her hand.

She didn't want him to know she'd been sobbing, but it was likely impossible to hide the evidence of how she'd spent the hours since they had parted.

"Because I wished to speak with you," he said solemnly, casting a look in Honoré's direction. "Your swan friend is menacing me. Do you think you might tell him to decamp? I've heard he bit the Duke of Bradford, and I have no wish to test the veracity of that particular rumor."

He was attempting to make a joke, and it wasn't a pun.

Charity's eyes narrowed as she studied him. "Why do you want to speak to me?"

Neville came nearer, and Honoré trumpeted, then hissed.

"The swan," he muttered.

Charity rose to her aching feet reluctantly, her ankle twinging as she did so. "I'll pay you a call later," she told

Honoré, giving him a final pat before she moved toward Neville, limping as she went.

"Your ankle," he said, frowning. "Why are you gadding about after spraining it yesterday? The doctor told you that you must rest to avoid exacerbating it."

Yes, the doctor had. But that had also been before her entire world had been torn asunder.

"I needed to be alone," she explained, wondering how he had come to her. "Who told you where to find me?"

"No one," he said easily. "I guessed."

"You thought I was swimming again, didn't you?"

"No, darling. I spoke with Lady Louise." His tone was gentle, his gaze tender. "She told me you had retreated from your bedchamber in haste earlier this morning and that you'd been distressed."

She froze, everything within her turning to ice. "What else did she tell you?"

Good heavens, did Neville know the truth as well? Surely she hadn't told him.

"Charity," he said, with such feeling that she knew at once.

He did know the true circumstances of her birth. And she couldn't bear the pity in his eyes.

"Don't say another word," she warned him, hurt welling up with a fresh round of tears.

Wincing, she turned away, her bare feet numbed and sore, her ankle paining her.

"Charity, wait. Curse it, you haven't any shoes on."

He caught up to her, taking her arm in a staying grasp that she could escape if she wished. But his touch was comforting. Heat swept over her, banishing the sadness and the anguish, the physical pain she was suffering too. Until she recalled that her love for him was hopeless now. His chief concern was his niece's future, and he couldn't achieve a proper match for Margaret if he continued to consort with a scandalous woman who had been born an illegitimate child.

"To the devil with my shoes," she bit out, frustrated. Hopeless. "I don't need them."

"Let me carry you to the bench," he said softly, his voice entreating.

He was looking at her as if she were Honoré, about to either hiss at him or bite him at any moment.

She sighed. "I can walk there."

"Of course you can. You can do many things on your own." He bent suddenly, sweeping her into his arms. "But you don't need to any longer, because now you have me."

Her stomach tipped at the swiftness of the motion, and she emitted a high-pitched sound of startlement, her hands settling on his shoulders for purchase. "But I don't have you. I *can't* have you."

And I love you, she thought miserably, but she didn't say the last aloud. Couldn't bear to.

"You do. You can." He started carrying her along the path, toward the bench they had sat on together what seemed a lifetime ago now. "I'm yours, Charity. Forever."

"What do you mean?" She studied his handsome profile, the golden stubble on his slashing jaw that glinted in the sunlight. "What are you saying?"

"I'm saying that from this moment on, when you run, run to me. I'll be waiting with open arms." He paused, then frowned. "But perhaps remember to wear some shoes first. You seem to have a remarkable fondness for flitting about in bare feet, and I can't help but think you'll step on a thorn one of these days."

She *had* stepped on a thorn, but of course she wasn't going to tell him that. Only Neville would think of something as practical as shoes, and she loved him for it. But still, she fought to understand his words, struggling to make sense of them. He seemed to be saying far more.

Or was that just hope making her think so?

"How will I run to you?" she asked as he carried her. "This house party is nearly over. We may never even cross paths again."

"Of course we will," he was quick to say. "Because I'm marrying you."

He was stern and unsmiling.

"You can't marry me," she countered. "I was born a bastard."

"You were born Lady Charity Manners, and you'll become Viscountess Wilton," he countered. "But I don't care how you were born, darling. It doesn't matter to me."

"You say that now, but what about Margaret? What about your sense of propriety? If anyone were to find out the truth about me, you'd both be ruined."

And she couldn't bear that. Hurting either of them was the last thing she wanted to do.

"No one will find out. No one knows, save you, Lady Louise, me, and your parents."

"They're not my parents." The truth still felt foreign. Like a dream. She could scarcely believe it.

They reached the bench, and Neville lowered her onto it with such gentle care that she almost started weeping anew.

He dropped to his knees before her, heedless of the dirt that would likely stain his impeccable tweed trousers. "I don't care who your parents are. They could be a chimney sweep and a costermonger. I want to marry you, and nothing and no one else signifies."

She studied his handsome face, longing to kiss him, love for him bubbling up and threatening to overwhelm her. "You're only saying that because you pity me. But you needn't, Neville. I knew what I was doing when I came to you last night. We both agreed that it would be one night only. What I learned this morning about my past doesn't change any of that."

"I don't pity you, Charity." He took her hands in his, raising them to his lips to press a fervent kiss to her knuckles.

"Of course you do. Why else would you come chasing after me when you learned the truth? Why else would you demand marriage when we've never spoken a word of it before now?"

He squeezed her fingers, his gaze intent. "Because I love you."

Her lips parted. For a moment, she could say nothing, think nothing. He had astounded her.

But then she shook herself from her stupor. "You don't love me, Neville. How can you? We've scarcely known each other for any length of time."

"How can I not love you?" He kissed her knuckles again. "You're intelligent." He punctuated the pronouncement with another kiss. "You're daring." Another kiss. "You're bold." Another. "You're strong." And yet one more. "You're everything I want in a wife and more, so much more. You charm angry swans and swim in lakes and read vulgar books, and every time I look at you, you take my breath away."

No one had ever said anything half so lovely to her. She would have fallen in love with him again for that speech alone.

"But what about Margaret?" she asked. "I'm scandalous. I'll never be able to free myself from the whispers surrounding that painting."

"Margaret will find a husband who loves her for who she is," he said, smiling up at her at last. "Or perhaps she doesn't want to marry at all, and she can follow us to the Continent."

"Us?"

"I thought that perhaps you might accept some company on your trip with Lady Louise," he added. "Since I'll be your husband."

Her grand tour. She had forgotten in this maelstrom. But Neville hadn't. And he loved her. Loved her so much that he was willing to take the greatest risk of all and make her his wife despite the scandal she brought with her.

"I haven't said I'll marry you just yet," she pointed out, softening as all the fight seeped from her.

"Then you had better say it, because I'm going to kiss you in the next five seconds, and I would prefer to be kissing my betrothed rather than a fellow guest at this house party."

She tugged him nearer with their joined hands. "I'll marry you."

He stopped when they were almost nose to nose. "You will?"

Charity didn't hesitate—Neville was the man her heart had been seeking. Not Ainsley. Nor anyone else. He was the other half of her, a man who appreciated her for everything she was and everything she wasn't.

A man who knew her scandals and her secrets and loved her anyway.

"I will," she said.

"Thank God." He kissed her then.

A deep, crushing, jubilant kiss that healed her wounded heart. She kissed him back, wrapping her arms around his neck and holding him close to her, nearly slipping from the bench into his lap in the process. He caught her, keeping her from falling, reminding her there was something else she needed to tell him.

Charity tore her mouth from his. "I love you."

His grin reached his beautiful eyes this time, before his lips settled back over hers, precisely where they belonged.

EPILOGUE

"What do you think of it, my love?" Neville asked from behind Charity as he slid his arms around her waist and drew her against him.

Charity melted into her husband's beloved, familiar form, surveying the vibrant oil painting in its gilt frame. *Venus at Her Bath* had been hung in a place of honor in Neville's chamber following his purchase of the artwork. A golden-haired goddess stared back at her, all creamy skin and bountiful hips and breasts. Charity did not fool herself that she possessed a fraction of the loveliness the painted Venus possessed, despite her husband's firm avowal that she was far more beautiful than the picture.

"I think it's fortunate indeed that you've chosen to hang it here instead of in the drawing room where my mother would see it," she said.

The word *mother* still felt a bit strange on her lips in relation to the woman she had spent her entire life knowing as Auntie Louise. But in the weeks following the revelation, Charity had come to understand her mother's decision. Unwed and carrying the child of a rake who had seduced and

180

abandoned her, Louise had found her options had not been plentiful.

She had hidden her condition and given birth to Charity in secret, and then her brother, the Earl of Sandrington, had taken Charity into his home and raised her as his own daughter. Thus, her mother had been able to remain a part of Charity's life, and Charity had not suffered the stigma of illegitimate birth. The man who had sired her—the third son of the Marquess of Glenfall—had died of consumption some years earlier, never having known he had a daughter.

Charity felt an odd sense of absence when she thought of the man; it was strange to no longer have a father after spending five-and-twenty years believing she had one. But she was also resentful toward the heartless cad who had abandoned her mother, leaving her with painful choices to make on her own. Charity no longer blamed Louise for keeping her parentage from her. She understood that her mother had been young and terrified, and she had done what she believed was in Charity's best interest.

Her mother had explained that she had always hoped to tell Charity the truth one day, despite her promise to the earl that she would never reveal it. But as the years had gone on, she had feared the revelation would cause a divide between them. Unexpectedly falling in love with Neville had taught Charity that life was unpredictable. Forgiveness had come with time, and following Charity and Neville's wedding and honeymoon, her mother had come to stay with the both of them and Margaret in Wiltshire.

"Hanging it in the drawing room would be terribly improper," Neville said, nuzzling her neck. "And besides, if any of the footmen looked at it, I'd have to challenge them to a duel."

Charity smiled, amused. "You do realize duels haven't been fought for decades, don't you?"

He chuckled and kissed the sensitive hollow behind her ear. "I'd do it anyway. Anything for Lady Wilton."

Neville was ever her champion and protector—the man she deserved, the man who had made her heart whole again. "Anything, you say?" Heat stole through her as she nestled her bottom against him and felt the stirring of his cock, rigid and thick.

They had retired for the evening, and she had something quite important she wanted to tell him. But it could wait. For now, she had something else in mind to occupy the both of them.

He nipped her earlobe in mock warning. "Within reason, darling."

She grinned. "You know how much I dislike reason. I far prefer passion instead."

"Minx." There was no heat in his voice. Nothing but the deep, mellifluous rasp of desire. His hands slid over her night rail, cupping her breasts through the thin fabric. "What is it my wicked hoyden wants of me?"

Her nipples went instantly hard.

"You like it when I'm wicked," she said, breathless as he kissed a path of fire along her throat and lingered there, making her knees go weak.

He rubbed his thumbs over the peaks of her breasts in slow, knowing swirls. "I do, indeed. It seems that ever since I fell in love with a mermaid, I'm perfectly dreadful at being proper as I once was."

Her head fell against his shoulder as he plucked at her nipples, molten desire pooling between her thighs, her sex already wet and aching for him. "A mermaid, you say? I'm certain I should be quite jealous that my husband has fallen in love with such a mythical creature."

He slid his hand down, over her belly, cupping her at the

juncture of her thighs through her nightgown. "She's cast a spell on me, I'll admit."

She gasped as he applied pressure, his fingers unerringly finding the tender bud hidden in her folds. "She has?"

"Mmm." He kissed her cheek. "She's all I can think about. All I want. Everything I need."

"I heard she was scandalous."

"Very."

"And far too bold."

"In all the best ways," he agreed, stroking her as his rigid length prodded her from behind. "I'm the most fortunate man alive to call her mine."

"She's quite fortunate as well," she managed breathlessly, hips stirring, her body achy and needy.

The painting was forgotten. So, too, the past and all her family secrets. Nothing existed but the two of them and the love and passion they shared.

He released her and spun her to face him, a glint in his gaze she recognized all too well. "Take off your night rail and get on the bed, love."

Oh. Desire pooled between her thighs. She liked when Neville was growly and commanding in the bedchamber. It did strange things to her insides. She grasped two fistfuls of her gown and tossed it over her head, leaving it to pool on the Axminster somewhere behind her. His heated stare swept over her appreciatively as she wasted no time in obliging him by draping herself on his bed.

He shed his dressing gown and then joined her, stroking his hands up her calves and parting her legs. His grin was pure, molten sensuality as his golden head lowered and he rained kisses along her bare skin. The pulsing in her sex turning into raw, achy need as his mouth traveled nearer to her center.

He blew a stream of hot air over her exposed flesh, teasing her further.

She wriggled, already desperate for him. They had been married two months, and each passing day only served to heighten their bond, both in the bedchamber and beyond.

"Please, Neville."

"Tell me what you want." He kissed each of her inner thighs.

"I want your mouth on me," she said.

His caresses moved over her hips, and then his hand found hers, their fingers twining together. "With pleasure, darling."

His tongue flicked over her pearl, and she nearly jolted from her skin. Charity could not contain her moan of approval. He lapped at her, knowing how to take her to the edge. Just when she was certain she could not sustain more torture, he sucked.

Her body bowed from the bed, seeking more.

And he gave her more. With his other hand, he hooked her hips over his shoulders, angling her so that his face was buried between her thighs. He feasted on her as if she were the most decadent dessert, his tongue delving deep into her channel, then slicking along her seam to toy with her pearl.

Her climax was upon her in an instant. Pleasure rocked through her, bliss radiating from her wet core as his eager tongue dipped in and out, devouring her. Their fingers tightened and held as the ferocity of her orgasm ebbed.

He rose to claim her, bringing their bodies together. In one thrust, he was fully seated, filling her. The closeness was exquisite. She held him tightly and found his lips, the taste of herself on his tongue. How she loved this man.

Together, they discovered their rhythm, bodies straining, seeking. His cock glided in and out, sinking deep. Their fingers remained laced as he made love to her, and when he left her lips to suck a nipple into his mouth, she reached her pinnacle, clamping on him hard as white-hot desire roared through her, stronger and even more intense than the crisis that had preceded it. On a growl, he pumped into her, and then the familiar wet warmth of his seed flooded her, prolonging the pleasure.

In the aftermath of their spent passion, they lay in each other's arms, hearts still beating fast.

Charity broke the silence first, reminded, now that her mind was functioning properly once more, of the news she had to tell him. "Neville?"

"Yes, my love?" He stroked the sensitive skin of her inner arm.

She took a deep breath—she had practiced this moment, the question, how she would present it. A silly little question she'd fashioned, just for him, as if it were a pun.

"What do you call a man whose wife is with child?"

"A father." His hand stilled, and he raised his head, his pale eyes searching hers. "Charity?"

She took his hand in hers and pressed them both to her belly's gentle swell. "We're going to have a baby, Neville."

"Oh my darling," he said, his countenance a mixture of awe and love so profound that she had to blink to clear away the furious rush of tears. "I could not ask for more."

"Nor could I," she said, her lips seeking and finding his as she wrapped her arms around him, drawing him close.

Neville kissed her sweetly, reverently, deeply.

He tasted like forever. He tasted like home.

～

THANK you for reading Charity and Neville's happily ever after! I hope you loved their heartwarming love story as much as I adored writing it. Our final friend is about to make her match. Read on for an excerpt from *Forever Her Scot*! Madeline and Lachlan Macfie are about to find their happily ever after in a marriage in name only that turns into something far more than either of them bargained for.

Please stay in touch! The only way to be sure you'll know what's next from me is to sign up for my newsletter here: http://eepurl.com/dyJSar. Please join my reader group for early excerpts, cover reveals, and more here: https://www.facebook.com/groups/scarlettscottreaders. And if you're in the mood to chat all things steamy historical romance and read a different book together each month, join my book club, Dukes Do It Hotter right here: https://www.facebook.com/groups/hotdukes because we're having a whole lot of fun! Now, on to that sneak peek of Madeline and Lachlan's happily ever after in *Forever Her Scot*...

Forever Her Scot
Dukes Most Wanted Book 6

American heiress Madeline Chartrand has a problem. Her matchmaking mother is determined to secure an aristocratic husband for her, despite her wishes to the contrary. Lachlan Macfie, the newly minted Duke of Kenross, has an even bigger problem. He's just inherited a moldering Scottish estate, crumbling castle and all, without the massive funds necessary to repair and run it.

Fortunately, Lachlan has the perfect solution—a marriage of convenience. It's a simple enough arrangement. Madeline gets the duke her mother hopes for, and Lachlan can restore the estate with the help of her vast dowry. All he has to do is convince the stubborn and delectable Miss Chartrand that marriage is the answer to both their quandaries.

Madeline doesn't want to wed anyone, least of all the burly Scot who trampled her train and spilled champagne on her gown at their first introduction. He's too tall, too brash, and too overwhelming. She doesn't even *like* him.

Until they're stranded alone together and Lachlan proves he's not just capable of protecting her from danger, but kissing her witless. Suddenly, Madeline finds herself facing an entirely new problem. She's falling in love with a man who wants a marriage in name only. But can she settle for a forever if she can't have his heart?

Chapter One

MADELINE WATCHED in helpless despair as her friend, Lady Charity Manners, was led away on the capable arm of Viscount Wilton. Across a gently rolling Yorkshire field they went, the sky a brilliant blue overhead, dotted with fat, puffy clouds. The perfect, bucolic scenery was distinctly different from the massive buildings and bustling streets of Manhattan. At any other moment, Madeline might have admired the beautiful pastoral landscape.

Might have even wished to capture it on canvas with the paints that had never been far from her side since she'd left her home in New York City.

But this moment was not an ordinary moment. And Madeline wasn't moved to capture the gallant departure of the golden-haired couple as they returned to the manor house so Charity's twisted ankle could be attended by a doctor. Because now, Madeline was alone with the towering man at her side.

"Ye dinnae care for my presence much, do ye, lass?" he asked, his Scottish burr seemingly more pronounced than ever.

And despite her intention to remain impervious, his low, deep voice slid over her like silk velvet.

Vexed, Madeline turned her attention back to Mr. Lachlan Macfie. He was not just impossibly tall, but broad of chest and shoulder, a massive mountain of a man who was brash and disturbingly attractive, his eyes bluer than the sky and his red-gold hair beneath a dashing hat worn in long waves that curled over his tweed coat. He made her stomach tighten with a familiar, tingling feeling she knew to ward off whenever it arrived.

"Why do you call me *lass*?" she asked sharply.

He grinned, and the dreaded feeling returned, because that carefree sinner's smile carved dimples in his cheeks. "What else am I tae call ye?"

"Miss Chartrand." She kept her tone icy, for she recognized his sort.

Mr. Lachlan Macfie was a fortune hunter if ever she had spied one. And Miss Madeline Chartrand, daughter to one of the wealthiest men in New York City, had most certainly seen more than her fair share of fortune hunters.

Oh, he dressed the part of a gentleman quite well, aside from his brilliant hair, which was far too long to be fashionable. But all scoundrels in search of an heiress for a wife made certain to look the part. Otherwise, their schemes wouldn't be successful. They were like foxes slipping into the henhouse, greedy and dangerous.

"Miss Chartrand," he repeated, still staring at her in a way that made heat rise to her cheeks.

It was his blasted accent that affected her, she decided. That and his height. He was a veritable giant. As a woman who was on the taller side herself, it was refreshing to converse with a man whose height surpassed hers by such a significant amount. To say nothing of the power hidden beneath his fine garments. He looked as if he were strong enough to tear a tree from the ground, roots and all, and then carry it over his shoulder like a twig.

Or to swing Madeline into his arms and carry her away as Lord Wilton was currently carting off Charity. But she didn't want that. Of course she didn't. Mr. Macfie was a fortune-hunting scoundrel.

"You should have carried Lady Charity back to the house," Madeline told Mr. Macfie, her voice curt. "You're larger and stronger than the viscount."

Rather than being duly chastened, however, Mr. Macfie's grin deepened. "I'm gratified ye noticed how strong I am, *Miss Chartrand*. However, I tried my best. Truth be told, I dinnae think Wilton wanted me tae carry his lady."

"*His* lady?" Madeline frowned, looking away from the Scot's smile and his dimples, which were somehow both irritatingly infectious.

He made her want to grin back at him.

Made her want to do more than that, in truth. Many things. Wicked things. Reckless things. Things that were foolish and stupid and would land her in a host of trouble. And that was why she couldn't afford to be alone with the man. Her own instincts weren't to be trusted. Her past attested to that; she'd nearly been duped by a silver-tongued confidence man with a beautiful smile and a penchant for saying everything she wanted to hear. She'd almost learned too late his true motive—not love for her as he had claimed, but an avaricious desire for her family's money. He'd certainly swindled enough of it from her before she'd realized the truth.

"Aye, did ye not notice the way he looks at her?" Mr. Macfie was saying, the words rolling from his tongue as if each syllable were a lover he caressed. "When I offered to take her back tae the house myself, I feared Wilton would bite me like a mongrel fighting over a bone."

"That analogy is hardly complimentary to either Lord Wilton or Lady Charity." She watched the viscount and her

189

friend disappearing into a copse of trees, wondering if she ought to chase after them.

Anything to keep from being alone with the man at her side.

"'Twas a saying of my dear sainted mother's. Forgive me. I didn't intend tae pay insult."

Madeline slanted another glance in his direction to find him watching her, his grin fading, the dimples blessedly subsiding. His legs were so long, his shoulders impossibly broad. She suspected he could carry three Lady Charitys across the field without even perspiring. The muscles beneath his tweed coat were pronounced and distinctive. She found herself wondering what they looked like, what they would feel like, so much barely leashed strength beneath her hands.

And then she promptly banished the curiosity, for it would only lead her down a perilous road. Handsome fortune seekers were not for her. She reminded herself of their initial meeting, when Mr. Macfie had stepped on her train and spilled champagne on her silk. He had known who she was. He'd crowded her with his big, brawny body, heat radiating from him beneath the blazing chandeliers and making her feel quivery and faint from his proximity. He had told her she was the bonniest lass in attendance with a familiarity that had made her pulse leap.

All reasons to dislike him.

"You are forgiven the slight," she allowed reluctantly, then sighed. "Perhaps we should follow them. There's no need for a picnic now that Lady Charity has injured herself, and there's likely far too much food in the picnic hamper for just the two of us."

To say nothing of the manner in which she had found herself in just the sort of indecorous predicament a confidence man would take advantage of. Just the two of them. Alone.

A frisson of something wholly unwanted trilled down her spine.

And then her stupid, traitorous stomach grumbled loudly and rudely.

She pressed a hand to her middle, mortified by the sound. Mr. Macfie laughed, the sound pleasing and low.

"It sounds as if yer stomach disagrees, Miss Chartrand." He offered her his arm. "Come. We're almost tae the picnic spot I had in mind. Ye'll ken why I chose it when ye see it."

Madeline glared at his elbow, not wanting to take his arm, not wanting to accompany him a step farther. But she was hungry, her stomach reminded her with another protesting grumble. And besides, she was impervious to the devilish charm of fortune hunters. She had learned her lesson. She could endure one picnic with Mr. Lachlan Macfie unscathed.

With great reluctance, she settled her hand on his tweed coat. "Very well, Mr. Macfie. I suppose we may as well eat before we return."

What could be the harm?

Mr. Macfie smiled down at her, his dimples reappearing. "Ye'll no' regret it, Miss Chartrand. That I promise ye."

As they continued up the hillside, a breeze carrying his masculine scent—shaving soap and a hint of fir—to her, Madeline couldn't shake the ominous feeling that she would.

Want more? Get *Forever Her Scot* now!

DON'T MISS SCARLETT'S OTHER ROMANCES!

Complete Book List
HISTORICAL ROMANCE

Heart's Temptation
A Mad Passion (Book One)
Rebel Love (Book Two)
Reckless Need (Book Three)
Sweet Scandal (Book Four)
Restless Rake (Book Five)
Darling Duke (Book Six)
The Night Before Scandal (Book Seven)

Wicked Husbands
Her Errant Earl (Book One)
Her Lovestruck Lord (Book Two)
Her Reformed Rake (Book Three)
Her Deceptive Duke (Book Four)
Her Missing Marquess (Book Five)
Her Virtuous Viscount (Book Six)

League of Dukes
Nobody's Duke (Book One)
Heartless Duke (Book Two)
Dangerous Duke (Book Three)
Shameless Duke (Book Four)
Scandalous Duke (Book Five)
Fearless Duke (Book Six)

Notorious Ladies of London
Lady Ruthless (Book One)
Lady Wallflower (Book Two)
Lady Reckless (Book Three)
Lady Wicked (Book Four)
Lady Lawless (Book Five)
Lady Brazen (Book 6)

Unexpected Lords
The Detective Duke (Book One)
The Playboy Peer (Book Two)
The Millionaire Marquess (Book Three)
The Goodbye Governess (Book Four)

Dukes Most Wanted
Forever Her Duke (Book One)
Forever Her Marquess (Book Two)
Forever Her Rake (Book Three)
Forever Her Earl (Book Four)
Forever Her Viscount (Book Five)
Forever Her Scot (Book Six)

The Wicked Winters
Wicked in Winter (Book One)
Wedded in Winter (Book Two)
Wanton in Winter (Book Three)

Wishes in Winter (Book 3.5)
Willful in Winter (Book Four)
Wagered in Winter (Book Five)
Wild in Winter (Book Six)
Wooed in Winter (Book Seven)
Winter's Wallflower (Book Eight)
Winter's Woman (Book Nine)
Winter's Whispers (Book Ten)
Winter's Waltz (Book Eleven)
Winter's Widow (Book Twelve)
Winter's Warrior (Book Thirteen)
A Merry Wicked Winter (Book Fourteen)

The Sinful Suttons
Sutton's Spinster (Book One)
Sutton's Sins (Book Two)
Sutton's Surrender (Book Three)
Sutton's Seduction (Book Four)
Sutton's Scoundrel (Book Five)
Sutton's Scandal (Book Six)
Sutton's Secrets (Book Seven)

Rogue's Guild
Her Ruthless Duke (Book One)
Her Dangerous Beast (Book Two)
Her Wicked Rogue (Book 3)

Royals and Renegades
How to Love a Dangerous Rogue (Book One)

Sins and Scoundrels
Duke of Depravity
Prince of Persuasion
Marquess of Mayhem

Sarah
Earl of Every Sin
Duke of Debauchery
Viscount of Villainy

Sins and Scoundrels Box Set Collections
Volume 1
Volume 2

The Wicked Winters Box Set Collections
Collection 1
Collection 2
Collection 3
Collection 4

Wicked Husbands Box Set Collections
Volume 1
Volume 2

Notorious Ladies of London Box Set Collections
Volume 1

Stand-alone Novella
Lord of Pirates

CONTEMPORARY ROMANCE

Love's Second Chance
Reprieve (Book One)
Perfect Persuasion (Book Two)
Win My Love (Book Three)

Coastal Heat
Loved Up (Book One)

ABOUT THE AUTHOR

USA Today and Amazon bestselling author Scarlett Scott writes steamy Victorian and Regency romance with strong, intelligent heroines and sexy alpha heroes. She lives in Pennsylvania and Maryland with her Canadian husband, their adorable identical twins, a demanding diva of a dog, and one zany cat.

A self-professed literary junkie and nerd, she loves reading anything, but especially romance novels, poetry, and Middle English verse. Catch up with her on her website https://scarlettscottauthor.com. Hearing from readers never fails to make her day.

Scarlett's complete book list and information about upcoming releases can be found at https://scarlettscottauthor.com.

Connect with Scarlett! You can find her here:
   Join Scarlett Scott's reader group on Facebook for early excerpts, giveaways, and a whole lot of fun!
   Sign up for her newsletter here
   https://www.tiktok.com/@authorscarlettscott

facebook.com/AuthorScarlettScott

x.com/scarscoromance

instagram.com/scarlettscottauthor

bookbub.com/authors/scarlett-scott

amazon.com/Scarlett-Scott/e/B004NW8N2I

pinterest.com/scarlettscott

Printed in Poland
by Amazon Fulfillment
Poland Sp. z o.o., Wrocław